"Taste t　　　　　　**aid, holding**

Those just might be the most romantic words that have ever been spoken to me.

Mandy tasted the sauce and licked her lips. "Perfect."

Leo grinned. "Good."

"Aren't you going to taste it?" Mandy asked.

Leo shook his head. "I don't need to. If Mandy Seymour, respected food critic, tells me it's delicious—then I know it's ready."

Mandy blushed and looked back down at the bubbling sauce. "So you trust me when it comes to tomato sauce?" she quipped.

Leo tucked a strand of Mandy's hair behind her ear.

"Among other things. Do you trust me, Mandy?" Leo asked in a low voice. Mandy stared up at him, enjoying the close proximity to him and the playful look in his eyes.

"Only when it comes to tomato sauce," she said with an impish smile.

BRANDY BRUCE

has worked in book publishing for nine years—editing, writing, reading and making good use of online dictionaries. She's a graduate of Liberty University, and currently works as a part-time nonfiction book editor. She and her husband, Jeff, make their home in Colorado with their two children, Ashtyn and Lincoln. Brandy loves reading, writing, watching movies based on Jane Austen books, baking cheesecake and spending time with her family.

BRANDY BRUCE

Table for Two

HEARTSONG
PRESENTS

Recycling programs
for this product may
not exist in your area.

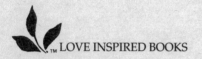

™ LOVE INSPIRED BOOKS

ISBN-13: 978-0-373-48703-5

TABLE FOR TWO

Copyright © 2014 by Brandy Bruce

www.Harlequin.com

Printed in U.S.A.

Taste and see that the Lord is good;
blessed is the one who takes refuge in him.
—*Psalms* 34:8

To my beautiful, capable, loving grandmothers,
Patricia Ann Brumble and Dora Sanchez Vela.
Thank you for your wisdom, courage, faith,
and love for family.

Chapter 1

Mandy Seymour held up one hand to hold off traffic as she dashed across the crowded street, wincing as the walk sign changed to Stop before she could reach the other side.

"Sorry, sorry," she muttered as the sound of honking horns followed her. She pushed through the revolving door of the Hyatt Regency hotel and rushed past the front desk. Taking a quick moment to look down at the brochure in her hand, Mandy took the next left and sighed with relief when she saw that the double doors to the conference room directly ahead of her were still open. She slid into the last row of seats and turned her attention to the speaker at the front of the room. Gabriel Romano. *The* Gabriel Romano—the well-known entrepreneur, chef and owner of three four-star restaurants, one in Los Angeles, and now two in Denver.

Mandy's mouth watered at the very thought of his famous tiramisu.

She caught the end of Mr. Romano's introduction as she shuffled through her purse, looking for a pen and a notepad.

How can I not have a pen? I always have pens—but of course, when I need one, there are none to be found.

Mandy ignored the disapproving voice in the back of her mind that always sounded just like her mother. *Mandy, why are you so disorganized? Mandy, when are you going*

*to be more responsible? Mandy, isn't it time you got your-
self together?*

"Here, take this."

Mandy looked up in surprise at the voice whispering
next to her. A man in a blue tailored suit with a silver tie
handed her a pen.

"Thanks," Mandy whispered back, accepting the pen,
her gaze lingering just a little too long on the man. His
dark wavy hair, jet-black eyes and olive skin were a nice
combination.

Don't even think about it, Mandy. He's probably married.

Was that her voice or her mother's in her head? Mandy
shook away the question and settled in her seat, eager to
be swept into Gabriel Romano's rise-to-success story, beginning with learning to cook in his grandmother's kitchen
during summers spent in the Italian countryside.

"So, why are you here?" the guy leaned over and whispered again.

Mandy barely glanced at him. *Okay, I know you're cute,
but I'm here to hear Gabriel Romano, so stop talking!*

Mandy shrugged and kept her eyes on her notepad. "The
same reason everyone else is—Gabriel Romano," she whispered, hoping her annoyance would register with the guy.

"So you're another admirer," he said.

It obviously *didn't* register with him.

"I'm a food critic," Mandy whispered in a rush as she
turned to look at him. "I'm doing a review of the new Romano's on Fifteenth Street tonight, so I thought I'd come
hear his story first."

A woman in front of them looked back, holding her finger to her lips. "Shh!"

Mandy's face burned with embarrassment and she concentrated once again on her notepad. The guy next to her
seemed unaffected.

"What time will you be there?"

"What?" Mandy asked, forgetting to whisper. The woman in front turned around again, glaring this time.

The guy leaned closer. "What time will you be at Romano's tonight?"

Mandy blinked, caught for a moment by those dark eyes of his. Why did he want to know? She looked back down at the notepad on her lap without answering.

"I'm Leo, by the way," the guy whispered.

Mandy sneaked another look over at him. He had a nice smile. But that didn't mean anything. There could be a lunatic lurking behind that nice smile.

"I'm Mandy Seymour."

What happened to the lunatic theory? I'm now having a conversation with a complete stranger—to whom I just gave my name—and I'm missing out on the speech that I came to hear!

Leo nodded. "Nice to meet you. What time will you be at Romano's tonight, Mandy?"

Mandy licked her lips and gripped the borrowed pen in her hand.

"Eight o'clock."

Leo winked at her. "Maybe I'll see you there," he whispered with a smile before leaving the conference room. Mandy watched him go, wondering where he was going and wishing she had asked him why *he* was there.

Leo Romano typed the name *Mandy Seymour* into his phone and waited for the search engine to give him what he needed. Within seconds, the first page of hits came up on the screen and Leo scrolled through, clicking on the third link.

Mandy Seymour, respected food critic for *Denver Lifestyle* magazine, recommends the Coffee and Crepes delicatessen at Twenty-Third and Mountain

View. Mandy was quoted as saying, "The service was impeccable and the breakfast quiche exceeded my expectations...."

Leo clicked off his phone and shoved his hands in his pockets. Even from the hallway, he heard his father's voice booming through the conference room. He could quote verbatim his father's speech, and while it was inspiring for the audience, Leo could only stand to hear it so many times.

He stepped closer to the open door, scanning the back row where Mandy Seymour sat, scribbling on her notepad. She'd rushed into the conference room, late, juggling a purse and shoulder bag; then she'd furiously rummaged through her purse until Leo had given her his pen. He'd been amused by her effort to ignore him and her frustration at his attempt at conversation. Wisps of brown hair had escaped the knot tied at the nape of her neck. Leo doubted that Mandy knew her scarf was haphazardly dragging on the floor when she'd rushed in. Everything about the woman shouted *scatterbrained.*

Still, scatterbrained or not, when Mandy dropped her pen and then scrambled to find it under her chair, Leo smiled from where he stood watching.

She's charming. In a clumsy, disheveled sort of way. Leo watched her sit back up and blow a stray hair from her face while she continued taking notes. *Not like Carol Ann. Clumsy and disheveled are two words that could never describe her.*

Leo's neck stiffened at even the thought of Carol Ann Hunt. It had been more than six months since she'd broken off their engagement and moved back to her parents' home in Chicago.

Leo leaned against the wall near the doorway and closed

his eyes, sending up a quick prayer for just a little more endurance.

Please help me get the new restaurant off the ground, Father. It's so important to my dad. He can't do this without me. And I can't do this without You.

The sound of laughter coming from the conference room broke his reverie and Leo looked up, glancing at his watch and knowing that the speech would be over soon. His father's voice echoed through the corridor and Leo couldn't avoid hearing the highlights of his father's life story. He listened as Gabriel Romano talked about discovering his passion—and talent—for cooking, marrying the love of his life and raising a family in Los Angeles, struggling financially to get his first restaurant off the ground. But through hard work, determination and a stellar reputation for good food, that first Romano's eventually thrived.

Gabriel told the audience that he hired his brother to be the manager and overseer of the restaurant while he concentrated on cooking, and a few years later he decided to move his family to Colorado. With the success of the Los Angeles Romano's, the opening of a second restaurant proved to be much easier. The restaurant on Franklin Street in Denver was an overnight success.

As the speech came to a close, Leo noted that his father hadn't mentioned that Leo would be the head chef, running the kitchen at the new Fifteenth Street location. He knew his father wanted to create more buzz by keeping the new chef's identity a mystery until the restaurant opened. That suited Leo just fine; he had enough on his plate without enduring the press and questions about his new role as head chef, along with the inevitable comparisons that would be made to his father.

As the crowd filed through the double doors, Leo moved back. From a distance, Leo could see Mandy Seymour make her way back down toward the lobby. Knowing she would be at the grand opening tonight, Leo would make sure everything—from the food to the service to the lighting—would be perfect.

Mandy took her time walking down the street toward Union Station. She planned to head back to her condo to work on her review of the mom-and-pop pizzeria she'd tried the week before. It was one of the things she loved most about her job—finding that diamond in the rough, so to speak. That little out-of-the-way place right outside of Denver that served amazing meat loaf or that tiny diner off Mosely Street that had the best cherry pie and home-made ice cream.

Not that Romano's could ever be described as a little hole-in-the-wall type place, with its marble flooring, out-door fountain, stone fireplaces, textured walls and magnificent murals—it was more than impressive. Mandy had been to the restaurant on Franklin Street a number of times. The Italian restaurant was practically a landmark in the area. But this latest Romano's promised new items on the menu, created by a new chef—obviously someone with Gabriel Romano's stamp of approval.

Mandy tightened her peacoat around her and picked up her pace as the wind brushed across her face. She wished she'd thought to wear a more substantial coat. It had been a mild January for Denver, but as a lifelong Coloradan, Mandy knew how unpredictable the weather could be.

The sounds of downtown Denver competed with the brisk wind as Mandy reached Union Station. She loved the energy of the mile-high city. She thrived on the lights, the noise, the crowds; living in a place bustling with people helped with the loneliness of living on her own.

Within seconds of finding a seat on the train, Mandy's cell phone rang. Just the sound of the Shirelles singing "Mama Said" told Mandy all she needed to know. Claire

Seymour was nothing if not predictable. Mandy held the phone to her ear.

"Hi, Mom."

"Mandy, are you still downtown?"

"No, Mom. I'm already on my way back home. Why?"

"I thought you said you'd call me on your way back to the Tech Center."

"I've only been on the train for about two minutes. I was going to call you once I'd been on the train for three minutes."

"There's no need to be snippy, Mandy."

Mandy watched the city fly by as the train moved. "Sorry."

"Good. Now, I'm cooking pot roast tonight, and I want you to come over for dinner. Your brother and Samantha are coming, too. Six o'clock."

"Mom, I already told you that I have plans tonight. I have to visit that new restaurant and then start my review. So I can't make it. But please tell Brian and Samantha that I said hello."

"I'm making pot roast!"

"Next time, okay?"

"Sunday dinner. I won't take no for an answer. I expect you in Evergreen by four."

"Fine. Tomorrow. Four o'clock. I'll be there."

"And I certainly hope you're wearing your good coat! It's freezing outside!"

"I know it is. See you Sunday."

Mandy clicked her phone off and leaned her head back against the cold window, ignoring the familiar wave of defeat that came over her whenever she talked to her mother.

As the train rattled to a stop, Mandy jumped up, swung her bag over her shoulder and braced herself for the cold wind. She allowed herself a little time to think about the mysterious Leo.

*He's Italian, obviously. Aren't Italian men famous for
flirting? Or maybe that's Greek men... Anyway, he probably didn't mean anything by it. And I'm sure he won't be
at Romano's tonight. He's too good-looking to be interested in me.*

Without a doubt, that last thought had her mother's tone.

*Don't think about Mom. I've proved her wrong so far,
haven't I? Here I am, living in the city with a job I love. I
haven't turned out to be the failure she feared I would be.
Okay, so I'm not married to a dashing, successful man and
I'm not the size-six, fashion-conscious, top executive she'd
wanted me to be. There are worse things in life.*

Mandy's shoulder bag fell to the ground, its contents
scattering. Mandy sighed.

Like being a walking disaster.

Chapter 2

"I told you, Ashley, it was nothing. He just asked me what time I'm going to be at Romano's." Mandy pushed the speaker button on her cell phone and set the phone on the bathroom counter before poking her head around the door to check whether the TV show she was watching was still on commercial.

A notepad with a half-written recipe lay on the coffee table in front of the muted television. Mandy's obsession with the Food Network usually resulted in notepads filled with amazing recipes, none of which she ever seemed to have time to make. When Ina Garten appeared back on the screen, Mandy told Ashley to hold on as she flew into the living room and jotted down the next step in making cheddar corn chowder.

Racing back to the bathroom, Mandy dug through her makeup bag, looking for her pale pink lipstick.

"I'm back, Ash. What were you saying?"

She waited for her friend to remind her again that at twenty-nine, Mandy wasn't getting any younger and she needed to take charge of her nonexistent love life. It was a speech Mandy heard nearly every time she and Ashley got together—or talked on the phone. But she didn't really mind. Ashley's natural tendency to be a fiercely loyal friend was something Mandy appreciated—and it helped Mandy overlook her other natural tendencies to be overopinionated and bossy.

As the social director of Redeemer Community Church's singles class, Ashley obviously considered herself an expert when it came to giving desperate women pep talks.

"Listen, honey, haven't you ever heard the phrase carpe diem? It means 'seize the opportunity' and that's just what you need to be doing, sweet pea." Living in Colorado for five years hadn't diminished Ashley's Virginia drawl. If anything, Mandy felt that the drawl was thickening.

"It means 'seize the day,' Ashley."

"Seize the guy, Mandy! You're not getting any younger! You've got to jump on these opportunities because they are few and far between. If a tall, dark and handsome Italian asked me what time I was going to be at Romano's, I'd tell him I could be there whenever he wanted me to be there."

A laugh disguised as a cough escaped Mandy. "Okay, okay. Well, I told him I'd be there at eight o'clock, and on the slim chance that he actually shows up, I should get going."

"Call me the minute you leave the restaurant. Or if things are going really well, take a bathroom break and call me. I want to hear every detail!"

Mandy stepped quickly down the sidewalk, hating the fact that there was absolutely not enough parking downtown. She paused for a moment to look over the front of the new restaurant. It was smaller than the Romano's on Franklin, but then, the Franklin restaurant took up a huge corner lot whereas this restaurant sat sandwiched between a boutique and a pub in one of the busiest parts of metropolitan Denver.

Even if this new Romano's had not been celebrating its grand opening, Mandy had no doubt that the line in front of the restaurant would be significant. The Romano's name alone would draw big numbers. She pushed her way through the crowd of people in the small waiting area and reached the hostess station.

"Table for one, please. Mandy Seymour. I have a reservation."

"Of course, Ms. Seymour. Right this way." The hostess gave Mandy a warm smile and motioned for Mandy to follow her.

Mandy wondered if the hostess knew she was a food critic. She hoped not. She preferred to experience a restaurant's staff and menu without the feeling that people were trying to impress her. As she followed the hostess through the restaurant, Mandy couldn't help looking around to see if the mysterious Leo was anywhere to be found.

You're here to work, Mandy. Stay focused.

"Here we are. Will this do, Ms. Seymour?"

Mandy nodded absentmindedly, frustrated that the dim lighting made it nearly impossible to scan the room for Leo.

"Um, there may be someone who asks for me. I'm not sure. Probably not." Mandy pursed her lips together to force herself to stop rambling.

"His name?" the hostess asked.

"Leo."

"Leo?" the woman echoed, her eyebrows rising. Mandy nodded, a bit confused by the woman's reaction.

"All right. Your server's name is Angelina. She'll be right with you."

Mandy slid into the booth before her, breathing in the scent of parmesan and fresh bread. She ran her finger over the white linen table cloth. The smooth sound of the violin could be heard throughout the restaurant, along with a low buzz of steady chatter.

The feeling of the place was so different from its sister restaurant. In fact, the stark contrast shocked Mandy. She took in the surroundings and listened to the music and came to the conclusion that she liked, even preferred, the quiet, sophisticated atmosphere. The colors of both the walls and the artwork—black and cream and white—were muted and soothing, much different from the colorful golden and deep purple hues found in the Franklin restaurant. The dim lighting made the room feel romantic. A large dining area was flanked by smaller sections, each with its own fireplace. Mandy herself sat in the quiet corner of a small section with a perfect view of a glowing fire.

Once the server had left to bring her a glass of water, Mandy pulled out a notepad and made a few notations about the restaurant's atmosphere and decor. She was studying the menu closely when Angelina returned.

"Have you decided, Ms. Seymour?"

"I'd like to know what you recommend," Mandy said.

"I'd start with the traditional Italian wedding soup. Then, if you like seafood, I'd suggest the Romano Lobster Magnifico."

"That sounds perfect. Thank you."

She'd grown used to dining alone. It was, after all, a large part of her job. But still, in a restaurant as intimate and romantic as this new Romano's, Mandy wished, not for the first time, that she wasn't alone. The waitress delivered her soup quickly—Mandy made a notation. She tasted the soup and found it to be quite satisfactory, if not outstanding. Angelina's recommendation for the main course, however, Mandy soon decided was her new favorite dish. She savored every bite of the succulent lobster and thick, tart cream sauce over linguine.

"So what do you think?"

Mandy's head jerked up, a stray strand of linguine hanging from her lips. She quickly wiped her mouth, her cheeks flaming. There stood Leo.

"You're a little late," she replied. He sat across from her without invitation. Mandy wanted to be annoyed, but the truth was that the sight of him made her heart leap—and her heart was so out of practice that she was okay with a little leaping.

"I know. Forgive me. I had to work late. And I'm afraid I can't stay long, but I did hope to see you. How was your meal? Wait, don't let me interrupt you. Please finish." He leaned back, his dark eyes fixed on her. He nodded toward the pad and pen on the table. "I see you're taking notes."

Mandy felt more than a little awkward, eating alone in front of this gorgeous stranger. She took a sip of water to buy a moment to collect her thoughts.

"Well, I definitely recommend the Romano Lobster Magnifico. It's incredible. And it's new. I've never seen it on the menu at the Romano's on Franklin. I'm thinking of ordering a second plate of it to take home with me."

Leo laughed. "Really? That good, huh? I'll have to try it sometime. Have you ordered dessert yet?"

Mandy smiled at the sound of his deep, warm, easy laugh.

"No, but I was thinking of—"

"Let me, Mandy. If I only have time for dessert, I want to make sure it's a worthy choice."

Mandy held both hands up. "By all means, you can make the worthy choice."

Angelina showed up as if on cue.

"We'll have the cherry cassata torte. And two cappuccinos." Leo looked at Mandy as though waiting for her to confirm his choice. She nodded.

"Yes, sir. I'll have that right out for you."

"How did you know that was on the menu?" Mandy asked as Angelina left them.

"The menu is posted outside. Didn't you see it?" Leo helped himself to a wedge of bread from the basket between them. "So, you're a food critic." he said.

"Yes, for *Denver Lifestyle* magazine. But I won't tell you

what I'm going to write about this restaurant. You'll have to read it along with everyone else."

Leo grinned. "I can promise you I will. But you did say that the meal was incredible."

"I did. And it was. But the verdict is still out on dessert. And I have to tell you—I'm definitely a dessert person."

"I would never have guessed," Leo responded.

"Oh, I am. In fact, I'm just a little heartbroken that I'm leaving without Romano's tiramisu. It's a favorite of mine."

"Yes. It's a favorite of mine, too."

Angelina returned with their coffees, one torte and two large spoons, placing the dessert between the two of them. Mandy stirred her cappuccino, wondering if sharing a dessert with a man she knew nothing about would be considered scandalous.

What am I thinking? I don't even know his last name! Of course this is scandalous! Wait till I tell Ashley.

"Taste this, Mandy. I think you'll like it."

Mandy took a small bite of the creamy torte and paused for a moment, the dessert nearly melting in her mouth.

"Oh, wow," she murmured. She looked up at Leo, who was watching her closely, his dark hair falling across his forehead.

"Well?" he asked. She smiled.

"What do you think 'wow' means, Leo? It's fantastic. You'd better hurry up or there won't be any left for you."

He picked up his spoon and took a generous bite, then glanced at his watch. "It was a worthy choice then."

Mandy didn't answer. She closed her eyes and enjoyed the next bite.

"I wish I could stay longer, Mandy. But I'm afraid I have to go. I really am sorry. Would you allow me to make it up to you another time?"

"You have to go? Back to work at nearly nine o'clock? Where do you work?" Mandy asked, biting her lip to stop the battery of questions flying out of her mouth. Leo looked down at his watch.

"I do have to get back to work. I usually…work evenings. I can tell you all about it the next time we see each other. But I'm running late now."

Mandy stared at him for a moment. "I know nothing about you, Leo."

He nodded. "I know. And I'd like to change that. How about breakfast tomorrow morning?"

"I go to church on Sundays," Mandy responded.

"So do I. We can meet before worship services. Is eight o'clock too early?"

You don't know this guy! Remember those "raving lunatic" thoughts? Then again, would a raving lunatic have such good taste in dessert?

Mandy looked him straight in the eye, searching for signs of madness. After a moment, she said, "Breakfast tomorrow morning. And if I leave it without knowing more about you, that will be the last meal we ever eat together."

Leo placed his hand over his heart as though he were wounded. "Well, it looks like I have this one chance to prove myself. Now, tomorrow morning—"

"You can meet me at Myra's Coffee House in Park Meadows. This time, it's my worthy choice."

The surprised but pleased look on Leo's face was almost better than dessert. Then, to Mandy's disappointment, his cell phone rang and he left in a rush. A few moments later Angelina returned, placing a plastic bag with two Styrofoam boxes on the table.

"What's this? I'm ready for the check, Angelina."

"Oh, no, Ms. Seymour. Your friend has paid for your meal. He also said that you'd like another plate of the Lobster Magnifico to go, along with a serving of the tiramisu. Here you are. I hope you have a lovely evening. It's been my pleasure to serve you."

Mandy looked at the plastic bag in shock, then back at Angelina. She tucked her notepad in her purse and thought of her review. "Wait, Angelina. Could you tell me the name of the head chef?"

Angelina froze in her step and looked at Mandy slowly. "The chef? Well, there were some changes regarding that this evening. I'm not sure if he'll be here on a permanent basis, so maybe I shouldn't—"

"That doesn't matter to me. It's just that the meal was excellent, so I'd like his name."

"He has Mr. Romano's full confidence. Most of the menu items will reflect our sister restaurant. There will be new items, of course. Like the one you had tonight."

Mandy's patience vanished. "Angelina, I'm a food critic for *Denver Lifestyle* magazine and website. I need the chef's name for my review."

Angelina sighed in resignation. "Leonardo Romano. You just had dessert with him."

Chapter 3

Mandy dunked her tea bag twice in her mug before dropping it in the sink and reaching for the sugar bowl. She tucked her cell phone in between her shoulder and her ear.

"I told you, Ashley, he lied to me."

"Which part was a lie?"

"Ashley!" Mandy's spoon clinked in her mug and hot tea splashed out on her hand.

"Calm down. You're still going to breakfast in the morning with him, right?"

Mandy made her way from the kitchen to the living room and sank into her favorite comfy chair. As usual, the Food Network was muted on the television. Mandy's love of cupcake competitions bordered on obsession. She watched as a woman decorated a Halloween-themed cupcake with tangerine-flavored icing and spiders made of licorice.

"*Mannnnndy?* Are you listening to me? Are you goin' or not?"

Mandy had no idea how Ashley managed to make her name stretch out to four syllables. She licked a drop of peppermint-vanilla tea from her finger before answering. "I'm going. But just to let him know that his little charade is up. Since the moment I told him I was a food critic, he's been manipulating me. Making me think he'd meet me at the restaurant because he was interested in me rather than because he works there. Making me think he'd chosen the dessert from the outside menu rather than because he invented the menu. Making me think that he was just a regular guy instead of the head chef of the restaurant I was reviewing!"

"I can see how you'd be upset," Ashley's calm tone grated on Mandy's nerves.

"Of course I'm upset!"

"You realize that he might actually be interested in you, Mandy. He's a good-looking, successful chef who goes to church. I really think you need to keep an open mind here."

Mandy didn't answer. An uninvited picture of Leo's handsome face and captivating smile crossed her mind. She remembered the wonderful sound of his deep laugh and the way he watched her as she tried the cherry cassata torte. Despite her best efforts, her heart fluttered at the thought.

"What about the review?"

"What?" Mandy asked.

"The review! The one you're writing up about his restaurant." Ashley's thick accent made *up* sound more like *uh-up.* "What are you gonna say?"

Mandy stirred her tea. "I don't know yet."

"The food was good, wasn't it?"

"It was delicious." Mandy sighed.

"Then you have to write a positive review."

"Ashley, let's talk about something else."

"Honey, you haven't been this worked up since skinny jeans came back—and we all know that was not a pretty sight."

"Skinny jeans are not a pretty sight! Especially on my thighs. I think they should be outlawed."

"Now let's not get started on *that* again. Find me as soon as you get to church and we'll talk about it."

"All right."

"And while you're there, do try to remember it's Sunday and you're a sweet Christian woman who's full of forgiveness."

Mandy chuckled in spite of herself. "You'd better pray for me."

"Believe you me, honey, don't I know it."

"So she was angry?" Leo echoed as he leaned against the countertop. His shoulders ached and his feet were killing him. It had been a busy night, which was good for the restaurant but for Leo—his exhaustion was reaching new levels. Angelina, one of Leo's first cousins, laughed as she began filling salt shakers.

"Of course she was! She probably thinks you were just trying to get a good review from her."

Leo squeezed the bridge of his nose and closed his eyes, hoping the headache that was taking over would pass soon.

"So tomorrow, be prepared. She's not going to like you." Angelina chuckled.

"I should have told her, I guess," Leo massaged the back of his neck. The restaurant had closed nearly an hour before but the noise level hadn't diminished. The wait staff had turned up the stereo as they cleaned. The sound of the music joined with the whirring of dishwashers running and people talking.

"It was a great opening night for us, Leo," Angelina said. "There were people all the way down the sidewalk, waiting even though it was freezing outside. Your father is proud of you, you know."

Leo nodded. He knew his father was proud of him. But at what cost? Exhaustion, stress, even fear—the emotions that came with the restaurant were heavy, and there were moments when Leo couldn't remember if he'd ever even wanted it for himself.

Just nine hours later, Leo pulled into the small parking

lot of Myra's Coffee House and squinted up at the sign. Morning had come too early. The twinge in his neck reminded him of the small amount of restless sleep he'd managed to get after he finally got home. Leo looked forward to a cup of hot coffee and hoped Miss Mandy Seymour would accept his apology and they could have a nice breakfast together. He just wasn't up for an argument this early.

Leo stood out front for a moment, surprised by the realization that the coffee shop was actually an old, renovated house that had been turned into a business. So many of the buildings in the Park Meadows area were new; the fact that this house looked aged made it all the more appealing.

When he walked through the door, a bell chimed and he watched as Mandy Seymour whirled around to face him. The look on her face made Leo doubt whether they were going to have a nice breakfast together. But he held out hope.

"Good morning, Mandy. It's nice to see you again."

"Hello, Leonardo *Romano*."

She had drawn out his last name as a pointed reminder that he'd kept that bit of information from her.

"Can I get a cup of coffee before I try to explain?" Leo asked. Mandy tilted her head, seemingly thinking over his request. It crossed Leo's mind that even as she stood there, obviously annoyed with him, she looked beautiful. Her brown hair was swept to the side in a thick braid and her light brown eyes studied him.

"Fine. I'll go ahead and order, as well."

"Fine. But I'd like to pay for both of us, if you don't mind. It's the least I can do," Leo offered.

"No. I'll get my own."

"Fine!" Her refusal to let him pay for breakfast frustrated him and Leo fought to push back his anger.

Is it really such a big deal? Angelina was right. This girl doesn't like me at all.

After ordering a cup of coffee and a ham-and-cheese croissant, Mandy stepped back and waited for Leo. He had an inkling that Mandy knew what was best on the menu so he ordered the same. Once they'd received their orders, he followed her to a table for two in the back corner of the shop.

After one bite of the croissant, Leo knew he'd made the right choice.

"This is delicious!" he exclaimed. The buttery, flaky croissant was stuffed with sharp, melted cheddar cheese and smoked ham. His anger subsided as he enjoyed the warm croissant. Across the table, Mandy nodded.

"I know."

Leo wiped his mouth and took a sip of his coffee, pleased by the strength of the house blend.

"Before you explain—or attempt to—" Mandy said, "first I want to thank you for dinner last night. But I'd like to pay you back."

Leo's frustration had been waning, but with that comment, it came back in full force.

"No."

"No?" Mandy looked taken aback.

"No. It was something I wanted to do. Just accept it as a gift and let it go."

"Accept it as a—"

"Let it go, Mandy."

They sat staring at each other. After a few tense, silent seconds, it seemed as though Mandy was choosing not to fight this particular battle. She nodded.

"All right, then. Thank you."

Leo knew it was his turn to speak, to explain.

"You're welcome. I apologize for lying to you—though I never exactly lied."

"Omission is as good as lying," Mandy countered, her voice quiet. Leo clenched his jaw.

"Okay! I'm sorry. I should have told you that my last

name was Romano, that I'm part-owner of the restaurant you were going to, and that I'm currently the head chef you were reviewing. But I didn't. Can you forgive me for that?" Leo knew his exasperated tone wasn't exactly communicating contriteness.

He could almost hear Carol Ann saying, *That's not an apology, Leo. When your heart is sorry, your words come out differently.*

The unwelcome memory of Carol Ann caused Leo to take a deep breath and try to steady his pulse. Thoughts of Carol Ann were the *last* thing he needed at this moment.

"Why didn't you tell me?" Mandy's voice was truly curious. Leo sipped his coffee again and thought before answering.

"If I had told you, from that moment the dynamic between us would have been different. You would have been more guarded, knowing that I was a chef you would be critiquing."

"I see. So deceiving me was for *my* benefit," Mandy surmised. Leo frowned.

"You're being a little unreasonable, don't you think?"

He watched as Mandy's eyes widened. "Unreasonable? Me? I… You…" Her sputtering would have been comical if Leo hadn't felt so incensed.

"Look, I came here to apologize to you. Obviously, you're not interested in hearing what I have to say."

"You're not really apologizing!"

At that moment, she sounded just like Carol Ann. And it took all Leo's strength not to pour out his frustration and anger on her. Even he knew at that moment, it would be misdirected.

Neither of them spoke. Leo couldn't believe this woman—practically a complete stranger—could incite such an emotional response from him. How many times had he dealt with angry customers and managed to keep his cool and defuse tense situations? With this woman, rather than defusing anything, he felt like a bomb ready to explode.

Under the table, Mandy's hands trembled. She and Leo were both breathing hard, the tension between them so thick Mandy could almost see it. Leo's excuse for lying to her was pathetic. She wished she'd never agreed to meet him for breakfast. Now she'd shared one of her very favorite places with someone who didn't really care about getting to know her better.

That thought, coupled with the anger she was feeling, was enough to make her want to cry.

Not here. Not in front of him.

Mandy swallowed with difficulty, trying to compose herself. She sincerely hoped Ashley had remembered to pray for her that morning.

"Leo." She cleared her throat, intending to redirect the conversation. She couldn't suppress the tiny hope inside her that this meeting might still be salvageable.

She forced herself to meet his gaze. Leo's dark eyes flashed with anger. She paused at the sight, and a sinking sensation of disappointment filled her stomach.

Mandy stood up and slung her purse over her shoulder. "Leo, I should go."

"That suits me fine," he answered.

She turned and walked out the door.

The moment Mandy stepped into the full sanctuary, she saw Ashley waving at her from across the room. The worship service had started and people were standing as the sound of praise music reverberated all through the building. Mandy dropped her purse on the pew next to where Ashley was sitting and stood next to her, hoping the music might quiet her spirit.

"So?" Ashley asked, leaning close to Mandy's ear. Mandy gave her a look and shook her head.

"Let's talk about it after."

"That bad?"

"Ashley!"

"All right! We'll talk about it after."

The moment the pastor stood at the podium, Mandy had a terrible feeling he was going to preach about forgiveness and loving your enemies and all the things that she just couldn't handle at that moment.

She held her breath as he opened his Bible and began speaking about faith, directing the congregation to a passage in Hebrews about great men and women of faith in the Bible. Mandy breathed a sigh of relief.

The moment the service ended, Ashley pulled Mandy into the church lobby and found a couch for the two of them to sit on.

"So, what did you do?" Ashley asked.

"Why do you assume it was my fault? He gave me some lame apology and acted annoyed when I didn't accept it immediately."

Ashley nodded. "Oh. So that was it, then, do you think?"

Mandy bristled. "Do you expect me to go out with a guy who treats me like that?"

"I just wondered if there was the teeniest hope that you two might try starting over."

"I don't think so, Ash," Mandy tried to keep the disappointment out of her voice.

Ashley looked at her with sympathy. "Gotcha. Well, you still have your review to write."

Mandy watched the people mingling in the lobby. "I know. I might start by describing the owner as rude—"

"Hold your horses, girl! You've got to stay professional about this."

Mandy didn't answer for a moment. "He certainly brings out the worst in me, doesn't he?" she finally said.

"Oh, I don't know about that." Ashley chuckled. "I was thinking that he brings out the fire in you. And in all the years I've known you, honey, I didn't even know there *was* fire in you."

Ashley's words played like a broken record in Mandy's head during the forty-five-minute drive to Evergreen. She tried to drown them out by turning the radio up as loud as she could stand.

By the time she turned down the dirt road that led to her parents' home in the small town of Evergreen, Colorado, she was desperate for some peace and quiet. Her younger brother, Brian, stood by the front door as she pulled into the drive.

"I wanted to warn you," Brian said as Mandy climbed the front porch steps.

"Oh, no. Is she in one of her moods?" Mandy groaned out loud as she thought about wasting an evening listening to her mother's criticisms.

"Let's just say she's already made it clear that she thought Samantha and I would be having a baby by now, that I would be promoted at work by now, that Dad would have fixed the kitchen sink's leak by now, and when it comes to you…"

Mandy shook her head. "Don't go there, Brian. I shouldn't have come."

Brian laughed. "Come on. You don't have to face her alone. And we both know that her complaints have more to do with her own dissatisfaction in life than they do with us. Try not to let her get to you." He threw his arm around Mandy's shoulders and gave her a squeeze. The small gesture was enough to give her the strength to walk through the front door.

"Mandy! Finally! I told you to be here at four." Her mother poked her head out the kitchen doorway.

Mandy just nodded. The clock on the mantle read ten after four.

"Do you want me to set the table?" she asked.

"Samantha did that already. Let's just eat. Everything's probably cold by now."

"Well, it smells great, Mom, as usual," Brian said light-heartedly. Mandy's dad opened his arms to her and she walked straight into them with a smile. He gave her a hug and kissed the top of her head.

"How's my girl?" he asked with a grin.

"I'm okay, Dad."

He cocked his head to the side and studied her. Mandy knew she wasn't fooling him. They filed into the dining room and Mandy sat down next to her sister-in-law and felt Samantha reach over and grasp her hand warmly.

"I'm so glad you came, Mandy."

"Thanks, Sam. It's good to see you."

After Brian prayed over the meal, Mandy asked her mother to pass the gravy.

"Not too much now, Amanda," her mother said as she passed the gravy boat. "You know how fattening it is."

Mandy gritted her teeth. *Then why do you make it?*

Samantha jumped in with a story about her and Brian's search for a new car, and Mandy was reminded, not for the first time, how lucky she had been in her brother's choice of a wife.

They managed to get through the meal, and after Mandy helped with the dishes, she walked out onto the back deck and breathed in the scent of the evergreen trees. The sound of the rushing river right behind the house filled her ears and soothed her. She'd lived in this house from the age of five until she'd left for college. And moments spent by the river had always given her peace when she most needed it. She could remember sitting on the deck, writing in her journal as a teenager. Fishing with her dad. Throwing rocks in the water with Brian. And always—except for the very coldest weeks of the year—she could hear the sound of the water rushing.

Mandy sat on the bottom step that led down to the riverbank and closed her eyes.

"I know," she said out loud.

"You know what?"

Mandy jumped at the sound of Samantha's voice. She looked up as Samantha sat down next to her. "Samantha! You startled me."

"So I gathered. Who were you talking to?"

Mandy looked back at the water. "God," she answered with a sigh. "He was reminding me that I should have treated someone with more grace this morning."

"Ah. He does that to me, too. Brian's usually the victim in my case. What about you?"

After contemplating for a moment, Mandy decided to confide in Samantha and told her the whole story of her disastrous meeting with Leonardo Romano. Samantha listened quietly until Mandy had finished with Ashley's perplexing comment about Leo bringing out the fire in Mandy.

"What do you think about that?" Samantha asked. Mandy shrugged.

"All I know is that every time I think about him, I feel angry."

"But have you thought about *why* you're angry? I mean, the real reason."

Mandy looked confused. "I just told you the reason. He wasn't exactly honest with me."

Samantha nodded. "Right. But I think the real reason you're upset is that you liked him. And you were excited at the thought that he liked you, too. Now you don't feel like you can trust his motives and you're disappointed. Am I right?"

Mandy threw a rock in the water. "You should have been a counselor, Samantha."

Samantha laughed. "It's easier to see things about other people than it is about yourself."

Mandy wrapped her arms around her knees. "I think you're right. I was disappointed. And I did like him. But it's over now."

"Except for your review," Samantha pointed out before standing up, dusting her jeans off, and heading back toward the house.

My review.

"Hey, Samantha?" Mandy twisted around. Samantha paused with her hand on the doorknob. "Did Brian bring his laptop?"

Samantha grinned. "It's upstairs."

Chapter 4

Leo dried his hands on his apron and then drew a spoon to his lips. After tasting the red marinara sauce, he nodded to his sous chef, Jeremy. "You're right. It needs more garlic. Then it should be perfect." Leo looked back at the row of cooks behind him. "Carlos, the heat under that soup needs to be turned down. Come on, people, pick it up! We're busy tonight. Get that bread out of the oven, Elliot."

Leo redirected his concentration to his work station. He leaned over the plate in front of him and delicately dropped parsley on top of a mound of steaming fettuccini.

"Hey, chef," Angelina said as she loaded her tray with the now-ready order. Leo waved her away.

"Don't distract me, Angie."

Angelina laughed. "Okay, I won't tell you that Mandy Seymour's review was posted online today."

Leo's head jerked up. "Today? Why didn't someone tell me?"

"I just did!" Angelina called over her shoulder as she pushed through the swinging door.

It had been nearly a week since Mandy had visited the restaurant, and Leo had checked the *Denver Lifestyle* website every evening looking for her review of Romano's. More than anything, Leo wanted to drop everything and read the review. But it was Sunday night and the restaurant was busier than usual. The long list of orders needed his attention first.

Four hours later, he had his first chance for a break and dashed to his office for a quick espresso and a chance to read Mandy's column.

I recently visited the new Romano's on Fifteenth Street in downtown Denver, which is located between AfterHours Pub and Grill and Primrose Boutique. Romano's white on black, classic outside decor was elegant and inviting. And a contrast to its famous sister restaurant on Franklin.

I couldn't help but feel impressed as I walked through the dimly lit restaurant. The sounds of Vivaldi, the glow of individual table lamps and the warmth from fireplaces placed strategically in small alcoves created a romantic atmosphere, perfect for conversation and an enjoyable dining experience.

At the server's suggestion I began with the Italian wedding soup, followed by Romano's Lobster Magnifico, a dish made specifically for the Fifteenth Street location. The traditional soup was not unlike others I've tried, though I would say that it was perfectly satisfactory and an excellent example of the way this soup *ought* to taste. The flavors blended together and the meatballs were moist and delectable, but did not overpower the texture and consistency of the soup.

I'm happy to say that I wasn't prepared for Romano's Lobster Magnifico. Just writing about this unique dish makes my mouth water. The chunks of lobster were cooked to perfection. The linguine was a perfect match for the heavy cream sauce, which in my opinion was nothing short of extraordinary. The thick texture and subtle tartness mixed with the sharp taste of parmesan—well, let's just say it was an experience I hope to repeat.

As for dessert, the cherry cassata torte was chosen for me and it was absolutely a worthy choice. The rich, decadent flavors and smooth, creamy consistency made this dessert absolutely heavenly. The head chef at this new Romano's is none other than Leonardo Romano, son of the esteemed Gabriel Romano. And while it's safe to say that the younger Romano is following in the footsteps of his father, I must add that, in my opinion, he is a superb chef in his own right. Check out Romano's on Fifteenth Street. You won't be disappointed.

Leo sat back slowly and exhaled. He hadn't realized his shoulders were tensed while he read Mandy's review, but he could feel it now. He reread the last few lines again and tried to decipher his feelings. He felt grateful, of course, for the positive and thoughtful review. But there was something else. A gnawing sense of guilt that he'd had ever since their last, unfortunate meeting.

And a quiet but consistent inward push to contact Mandy and apologize.

A tap on the door interrupted his thoughts. Leo called out for whoever it was to come in.

"In your office? Shouldn't you be cooking?"

Leo looked up at his father and smiled. "Hey, Dad. I couldn't help it. A review was posted today and I had to read it."

"Positive, I hope?" his father said as he sat down across from his son.

"Glowing."

"Good, good. Though I'm not the least bit surprised."

Leo saw that his father looked tired. Out of habit, his

eyes gravitated to his dad's hands for signs of tremors. He saw his father's right hand jerk slightly.

"How are you feeling tonight, Dad?"

"I'm all right. A little worn out, I guess. But Isa called and wanted your mother and me to join her for dinner at the newest Romano's and I wasn't about to say no. Not when Leonardo Romano is cooking." His dad grinned at him and Leo chuckled.

"I can't believe Angie didn't tell me you were here. Maybe she did and I just didn't hear her. The kitchen's been busy tonight. So what did you have?"

"Farfalle with mushrooms—one of your new additions. It was excellent, Leo. I want you to consider putting it on the menu at the Franklin location."

Leo smiled. "I'll think about it."

"Isa and your mother are having dessert now. I wanted to talk some things over with you. I'll wait till closing, of course."

Leo stood up and shook his head. "There's no need for that. Jeremy can take over for me in the kitchen. Let me just go check on things and I'll be right back. Can I bring you anything?"

"Some water, that's all."

Leo rushed to the kitchen and found that the orders were slowing down. His staff had everything under control. Leo left instructions for Jeremy and headed back to his office with a bottle of water.

His dad took the bottled water and this time there was no mistaking the shudder in his hand.

Leo tried to keep his face devoid of emotion, hiding the anxiety he felt every time he saw his father shake. Gabriel Romano had been diagnosed with Parkinson's disease four years earlier, but the symptoms had been nearly nonexistent for a long time. Over the past six months, however, the effects of the disease had started to manifest more quickly.

"So what's up, Dad? Everything going well at the Franklin Romano's?"

His father waved his hand absentmindedly. "You know it's a well-oiled machine. I rarely have to even show up. My staff is excellent. But even so, your mother—well, your mother thinks the stress of the restaurant is starting to affect my condition."

Leo frowned. "She's right. You know stress triggers the symptoms."

"The symptoms are coming regardless. Living life on my sofa won't help me."

Leo tightened his lips to keep from responding. He'd learned from experience that arguing with his father never helped.

"What are you thinking, then?" Leo asked as calmly as possible.

His dad sighed and leaned forward, his elbows on his knees. "I've decided to sign over the Los Angeles restaurant to your uncle. He's been running it for years now, anyway, and has wanted to buy me out. I don't see the point in waiting."

Leo nodded, thankful for his father's decision. "Uncle Tony deserves that restaurant. Releasing it to him entirely will free you from the stress of dealing with the finances, overhead—everything. It's a good decision, Dad."

"And I'm signing over both the Franklin restaurant and this one to you. My attorney is drawing up the paperwork to put everything in your name."

A sinking feeling washed over Leo. "Dad, I don't think I—"

"Your mother wants me to go ahead and do this, Leo, and there's no reason not to. It's been my intention all along. Your sister isn't interested in running the restaurants. She wants you to have them. You can hire a chef for this Romano's and concentrate on managing both. Or you can continue being head chef here. There are plenty of people in place to help you with whatever you want to do."

Leo couldn't speak. How could he tell his dad that he didn't want the responsibility? That it was already too much for him? That a million restaurants couldn't fill the void left by his broken engagement? That between his father's deterioration and the stress of the restaurants, he'd have nothing left?

He looked down, silent.

I will never leave you.

It was a scripture that he'd learned years ago. And while he didn't feel any less anxious, he felt relief at the reminder that God would be with him every step of this journey. No matter how difficult.

"All I can do is try, Dad. If you want to turn the restaurants over to me, I'll do the best I can. I know the restaurants are your legacy."

His father leaned across the desk and covered Leo's hand with his.

"Listen to me, son. The restaurants have been my livelihood. Cooking has been my career and one that I've thoroughly enjoyed. But *you* are my legacy, Leonardo. You and Isabella. Don't ever forget that."

Late Tuesday afternoon, Mandy unlocked her car and threw her purse on the passenger seat.

"Mandy!"

Beth, the office administrative assistant, ran to her, a vase filled with wildflowers bouncing in her arms.

"I can't believe you're still here! I thought for sure you'd gone home!"

"Careful," Mandy said, noticing the water that had splashed from the vase onto Beth's arm.

"Oh! Never mind that. These are for you! They were just delivered to the office!"

Mandy's mouth fell open. "Who would send me flowers?"

"Well, there's a card—but don't worry! I didn't read it."

Mandy took the bouquet from Beth.

"Thanks, Beth."

Once in the car with the flowers secured in the passenger seat, Mandy ripped open the card. It read:

With gratitude,
Leonardo Romano

Mandy tried to talk herself out of feeling disappointed.

He wanted to thank me for the positive review. It's probably just a courtesy. But couldn't he have said something a little more personal on the card? Or even, gasp, an apology? All he has to say to me is "With gratitude"? Really?

By the time she reached her apartment, she was caught between feeling appreciative of the flowers and growling that Leo's attempt to thank her was as feeble as his attempt at an apology at Myra's Coffee House.

Still, perched on her kitchen counter, the wildflowers did look nice. Mandy was still in her work outfit, staring at the flowers when a knock at her door made her jump.

She checked the peephole and froze. There stood her mother and Samantha. Mandy did a quick scan of her apartment and her heart sank. She'd stayed up late working the past several nights, trying to hit a handful of deadlines that all seemed to come at once. Laundry waiting to be folded lay piled on the sofa. Dishes in the sink needed to be washed. Mail was scattered on the coffee table.

She was tempted to do a quick cleanup, but another, impatient knock stopped her.

Mandy threw open the door. "Mom! Samantha! This is a surprise!"

Her mother brushed past her. With an apologetic look,

Samantha walked through the door and leaned over to Mandy.

"Why haven't you answered your phone?" she whispered furiously.

"My phone? What are you talking about?" Mandy whispered back through clenched teeth, a fake smile plastered on her face.

"Samantha and I were shopping at Park Meadows. We want you to come to dinner with us," her mother stated as she inspected Mandy's apartment. Mandy didn't even have to look at her mother to imagine the disapproving look on her face.

"It's been a busy few days," Mandy said, digging through her purse for her phone. She wanted to kick herself when she saw that she'd accidentally turned the ringer off. She scrolled through her call history.

10 missed calls
4 missed text messages
All from Samantha.

"Where did you get the flowers?" her mother asked.

"They're beautiful," Samantha added.

"Yes, but *who* sent them to you?" her mother repeated, obviously not about to let the question slide.

"I wrote a positive review for a restaurant so the owner sent me flowers as a thank-you."

"That was nice," Samantha said. Mandy could tell Samantha was dying to ask whether the owner was Leonardo Romano, but thankfully, she didn't say anything.

"Good grief, Mandy. When was the last time you swept your kitchen floor? Maybe we should stay here and help you clean up. This apartment looks atrocious," her mother said as she eyed Mandy's leftover breakfast on the kitchen table.

Mandy swung her purse over her shoulder. "C'mon. I'd love to have dinner with the two of you. Let's go. Have you picked a place? What are you in the mood for?" she rambled as she moved her mother in the direction of the door.

Twenty minutes later the three of them were seated at P.F. Chang's.

"Mandy, when was the last time you had your hair cut?" her mother asked. "I think I can see split ends from where I'm sitting. Do you have a good hairdresser around here?"

Mandy felt her jaw tighten.

Let it go. It's just dinner and then she's going back to Evergreen. Don't let her get to you.

"It has been a while since I had a haircut. I should probably do that soon. Are you getting the chicken lettuce wraps, Samantha?"

Samantha jumped in. "Absolutely. Want to share an order of dumplings?"

Her mother shifted to the topic of Brian and Samantha's upcoming anniversary, so Mandy was spared from having to make small talk and pretending not to be offended by her mother's critical comments.

But halfway through the meal, pretending started to get old.

"Mandy, I've told you before that you wear too much black. I know it's slimming, dear, but it seems like every time I see you, you look like you're in mourning. You should introduce some color into your wardrobe."

Mandy looked down at the black blouse she was wearing. The day before she'd worn a red sweater and gold scarf. Today she'd worn black. Mandy narrowed her eyes.

"Mom, do you have to—"

"Where's our waiter?" Samantha interrupted. "I'm so thirsty."

"There he is," Mandy's mother said and waved the waiter over.

Mandy took that opportunity to practice the breathing

exercises she'd learned during the first, and last, yoga class Ashley had dragged her to.

By the time Samantha and her mother hugged her good-bye and left for Evergreen, Mandy felt as if she'd battled a silent war. Not quite ready to go home, she drove across the street to the mall. She grabbed a cappuccino and sat in a leather chair by the fireplace outside of Neiman Marcus. It was at times like this that she hated going home alone. She wanted someone to vent to, someone who cared about her feelings.

But she'd have to settle for a crowd of strangers. With a sigh, she flipped up a handful of her hair and inspected it.

Split ends. Just like her mother had said.

Chapter 5

At five minutes after eight the following Friday night, Mandy sat in her car in the Franklin Street Romano's parking lot, giving herself a pep talk. *Of course* Beth would choose Romano's as the restaurant where their editorial team would celebrate her birthday. Mandy knew she had to go in and comforted herself with the reminder that Leo would certainly be at the Fifteenth Street restaurant, so there was no danger of her running into him. Even though, despite her best efforts, the thought of seeing him again intrigued her.

Tiramisu. Think tiramisu, Mandy. Leo is nowhere near here. You can go in, have a fantastic dinner, including dessert, and go home.

But the moment she walked through the door, Mandy got the feeling that things weren't going so well. The hostess looked overwhelmed and frantic and servers were dashing back and forth between complaining customers and the kitchen. After waiting longer than necessary, Mandy was directed to the table for eight that Beth had reserved earlier. Beth and her boyfriend were already there, along with Mandy's supervisor, the director of their department and a few other columnists. Mandy sat down.

"What's going on?" she asked, watching as a couple nearby asked to see the manager.

"They've got to be short-staffed or something. It seems like a lot of people have been waiting a long time. And I overheard one of the waiters tell someone that they've run out of calamari. Calamari! How is that possible? It's an Italian restaurant!" Beth answered.

"A waitress dropped a bottle of wine and it shattered all over the floor. That was terrible. She started crying and everything," Mandy's supervisor, Ann, said, her eyes on the menu in front of her.

"I'm sorry for the wait."

Mandy looked up as their server began filling their goblets with water. "We're running short on staff this evening and have had to call in a second chef. But things are getting back to normal and I'm here to make sure that you have an excellent dining experience."

"A second chef?" Mandy echoed. "Would you mind if I asked who?"

The server studied Mandy before pulling out her notepad. "Mr. Leonardo Romano is our chef this evening. I can assure you, he's the best."

Mandy felt her heart rate double.

While the wait for their orders was long, Mandy didn't care and could hardly concentrate on the conversation around her. She kept thinking that Leo was in the same building, probably stressed and overwhelmed. And there was nothing she could do about it.

Was there?

Of course not. He doesn't know I'm here, and if he did, he'd probably be more frustrated and anxious, even though I'm not here to critique anything. I just wish I could help in some way. Why do I care? It's not like this has anything to do with me. It's not like he *has anything to do with me.*

Two hours later, her coworkers were packing up to leave

and Mandy was stalling, not sure what she was waiting for, but not ready to leave. She told everyone to go on without her as she dawdled in the lobby.

"Miss? Can I help you?" Mandy turned around to see the exhausted hostess. The lobby was finally empty but there was another half hour before closing.

"I was wondering if I could help—it's just, well, you seem short-staffed and I'm a...friend of Leonardo Romano's and would love to help him out here if I could."

"Oh, no, we couldn't—" At that moment, the hostess was interrupted by a crashing sound. She squeezed her eyes closed. "This is *not* our night. We do not have enough people. Okay, I need to go check on whatever just happened, would you mind just sort of manning the hostess station until I can get back here? What's your name?"

Mandy was already taking off her jacket. "I'm Mandy, and I can absolutely watch over things here. You go."

The hostess hesitated. "My name is Liz. Nice to meet you. But I don't know..."

"It's okay. Like I said, I can talk to Leo about it later and tell him I insisted on helping."

The hostess finally nodded and dashed off in the direction of the crashing sound.

Fifteen minutes later, Liz returned. "We close in ten minutes so we won't be seating anyone else, but we have to keep the doors unlocked. Thanks for waiting."

Mandy smiled. "No problem. So, what happened tonight?"

Liz rolled her neck and stretched her arms. "Too many people called in sick or couldn't make it for whatever reason. The worst problem was when our head chef had to leave. There were so many orders that our sous chef was beyond overloaded. Everything that could go wrong—did go wrong. Things settled down once Leo arrived—since you're friends with him, I'm sure you know what an amaz-

ing guy he is. He came in and—" Liz snapped her fingers
"—took over. He's so much like his dad."

Mandy studied the floor, trying to ignore Liz's comment about her being friends with Leo and him being an
amazing guy.

"What do you have to do after you lock up?" Mandy
asked as another couple left with takeout bags in their hands.

"Normally I would just leave. But since there are so few
of us here, I'll need to help clean up. As long as I don't have
to help clean the kitchen, I'm okay," Liz said with a laugh.
"I do *not* like dirty dishes."

"Can I help you clean up?"

"Oh, no—"

"Come on. How much damage can I do? Like I said,
Leo's my friend. He'll be fine with it, I'm sure. So don't
even mention it to him right now." *Or ever,* Mandy thought
to herself.

"We're cleaned out, Liz!" someone shouted and Liz
sighed with relief. She pulled her keys from her pocket
and locked the wooden double doors.

"Do you want to sweep the lobby while I start on the
bathrooms?" Liz asked, glancing back at the kitchen. "I
can go ask Leo—"

"I can absolutely sweep in here. You go get the broom
and I'll explain to Leo when I see him."

Mandy knew it was the weariness in Liz that gave in.
She retrieved a broom for Mandy and headed off to clean
the bathrooms. Once she finished sweeping, Mandy took
over cleaning all the mirrors in the lobby.

"Thank you *so* much, Mandy," Liz said as they lugged
the cleaning equipment to the storage closet. Mandy glanced
around nervously, hoping they wouldn't run into Leo. She
couldn't bring herself to ask Liz whether he'd already left.

"I was glad to do it. The Romanos are a very special
family," Mandy said honestly. Liz nodded.

"They really are. I've worked here for four years, ever since I got out of high school. And I've never met a family like the Romanos. They are so hardworking, so kindhearted and so loyal to each other. They're the kind of family I wish I'd been born into."

Mandy let those words sink in. This was Leo's family Liz was talking about. More than that, this was *Leo*—hardworking, kindhearted, loyal.

Mandy shook off those thoughts and threw her arm around Liz's shoulders. "I enjoyed working with you, Liz."

"Hey, if you ever need a job…" Liz quipped with a grin. Mandy laughed.

"Keep me in mind."

Leo decided to do a last-minute walkthrough of the restaurant, just to make sure everything was in perfect shape for tomorrow's workday. As he walked through the dining rooms, he couldn't quite decide whether he was starting to feel ownership of the restaurant that was now his, or if his concern was merely the fact that it was his father's restaurant and a source of pride and joy for him.

One of the hostesses, Liz, hovered over the host station.

"Liz, what are you still doing here?"

She looked up in surprise at him. "I was in my car when I realized I'd forgotten my watch. I'm not working again till Tuesday so I had to come get it." She strapped her watch on her wrist. "By the way, your friend was such a big help to me tonight."

Leo was confused.

Am I supposed to know who she's talking about?

"My friend?"

Liz nodded, walking back with him to the rear exit of the restaurant. "Yeah, Mandy. She was here during all the chaos and stayed after her party left to help out. She insisted, really. She said that you were her friend and she wanted to help and you wouldn't mind. I hope I—I mean, we were so short-handed and I thought—" her voice trailed off.

Leo saw in Liz's eyes the dread that she'd possibly just made a big mistake.

"No, it's fine. But next time that happens, run it by me or Adam first, okay?"

Liz sighed in obvious relief. "Absolutely. I'm sorry I didn't run it by you tonight. We were just so swamped and Mandy was so sure you wouldn't mind."

Mandy.

"She's really great, chef."

Leo didn't respond but Liz kept chattering.

"I mean, she wouldn't take no for an answer. And she pitched in with everything. She wiped down the mirrors and swept…she said that the Romanos are a very special family."

"She said that?" Leo said suddenly.

Liz nodded with a slightly mischievous grin. "I think she really likes you. Goodnight, chef!"

Leo watched as Liz trotted over to her car and left.

Mandy said she was my friend? She stayed after hours and helped clean my restaurant? She told Liz that my family's special? What's going on here?

Confusion clouded Leo's thoughts.

Instead of leaving, he turned around and went back into Romano's. Alone in the restaurant, he turned a few lights back on and walked through the dining areas slowly, taking note of every detail that his parents had personally chosen.

On every wall, he could see his mother's touch. He walked through the enormous kitchen and sat in a corner chair. In his mind, he could see himself as a child—not in this kitchen but the one in his family's home in California— and he could hear his father singing as he chopped onions and tomatoes and garlic and bell peppers. Leo had grown up around the pleasing aromas of his father's own culinary creations. Those smells reminded him of home, family, love, happiness. He could picture perfectly his dad's steady hands pulling homemade bread from the oven, the scent filling the house and making Leo's stomach rumble.

And he could hear his father's voice saying, *Leo, see this fine bread? Jesus is the bread of life. Do you know why I love the fact that Jesus is referred to as the bread of life? Because not only does bread sustain us, which it does, of course, by giving us life, keeping us going, and giving us strength; but the beauty is that it also tastes good. It smells good. It is good. Bread is for us to enjoy. It's a blessing, a comfort. That's who Jesus is, Leo. Never forget. He's the bread of life. Taste and see that the Lord is good!*

Leo rolled those words back over in his mind. His father had such unwavering faith. And yet despite that faith, his health was deteriorating. Eventually, Leo would lose him. That realization made Leo's own faith wobble and wane. *Why* was God letting this happen? Leo wanted to yell and pound his fists on the countertop. But he didn't. He wasn't sure if venting his frustration was considered prayer, but his thoughts poured from his heart, directed straight to God.

While I'm on the subject of why—*why did Carol Ann walk away from our relationship? Why did I waste years on loving her when it wouldn't last? Why do I feel pushed into a corner, living a life that feels as though it's been chosen for me?*

Leo sat in silence, waiting for answers that never came.

Chapter 6

Monday evening after sitting in strategy and update meetings and catching up on two reviews, Mandy put her coat on and prepared to go home and unwind.

"Mandy! Wait up!"

Mandy stopped by Beth's desk.

"Beth? What's up?"

"You just got a call from Leonardo Romano. I didn't want to give him your cell number without your permission."

Mandy's eyes widened. "What did he say? What did he want?"

"To talk to you! But since you were in a meeting and I wouldn't give him your number, he left his and asked if you would call him. Here, take this." Beth handed Mandy a yellow sticky note. "Call him. He sounds nice."

Mandy looked down at the note in her hand and her heart pounded.

The next morning, Mandy drank a cappuccino and glanced again at the yellow note on her kitchen table. She planned to spend the morning writing reviews from the comfort of her home in the comfort of her pajamas. A rat-tat-tat knock sounded at her door, followed by Ashley barging into her apartment.

"I brought doughnuts!" she called out, dropping the box on the counter and helping herself to the cappuccino maker.

"I haven't called him yet."

"What?" Ashley's jaw dropped. "I thought you were going to call him last night."

"It seemed too desperate to call him immediately."

With a frustrated grunt, Ashley pulled out a chair from the table and plopped down. "You *are* desperate, honey. Remember?"

"No, I'd forgotten. Thank you for reminding me," Mandy retorted.

"No problem," Ashley replied sweetly. "Now, call him."

"Right now?"

"Now or never. C'mon, I'll help you through it."

Mandy seriously doubted whether Ashley would be any help, but she punched the number into her cell phone and waited.

"Hello?"

"Leo?"

"Is that him?" Ashley whispered. Mandy held up her hand to silence her.

"Mandy?"

"It's me," she replied, then whispered to Ashley, "It's him."

"So you got my message," Leo said. Mandy thought he sounded a little nervous.

"What did he say?" Ashley whispered again. Mandy rolled her eyes.

"Nothing!" she whispered loudly.

"Um, are you talking to me?" Leo asked. Mandy slapped her hand across her mouth and then mouthed to Ashley, "Stay here," and disappeared into her bedroom.

"Sorry, no, I wasn't. But I am now. Yes, I got your message. I was glad you called." Mandy sat on the bed and traced the patches on her quilt with her index finger.

"You were?" he sounded unconvinced.

"Well, yes. Thank you for the flowers."

"Thank you for such a good review."

"No problem. It was the truth."

"Well, I appreciate it."

"You're welcome." Mandy's words were followed by the most awkward silence she'd ever experienced.

"I guess—"

"I was wondering—"

"What were you going to say?" Mandy asked quickly.

"No, you go ahead," Leo said.

"No, you," Mandy insisted, feeling as if they were in high school.

"I'm sorry about the way things ended between us, Mandy. I'm not usually so temperamental."

Mandy could hear the sincerity in his apology this time. And she felt all the anger seep out of her. "Me, either. And I'm sorry, too."

"So what do you say? Should we try one more time?"

Mandy laughed. "I'm willing if you are."

"Excellent. I'm afraid that weekend evenings are my busiest. Would tomorrow evening work for you?"

"Tomorrow would be great, Leo. Where would you like to go?"

"Your choice, but I'm paying."

Mandy smiled. "Deal."

Wednesday morning, Leo sat nervously by his father, watching him sign the paperwork that would undoubtedly cause Leo's current stress level to skyrocket. The room was silent except for the family's attorney turning page after page, showing Gabriel where to sign in the enormous stack of papers. Leo knew his turn was coming and it made him sweat.

Should I sign? It's not like I really have a choice at this point. I told Dad I'd do this for him. It's such a big under-taking, though…and I know restaurant life. It takes over. I'll never have any personal time.

Leo's attention jerked back to his father as his pen fell to the floor. He checked his dad's hands and felt pain as he saw how badly they had started trembling.

"No, no!" his father insisted, when the attorney offered to take a break. "I want to finish this. I'll be fine."

Leo remained silent. Numbness seemed to spread through him, which he preferred to feeling overly stressed, fearful, nervous and resentful. For some strange reason, Carol Ann entered his thoughts. He thought of the night she'd stood in front of him, crying, as she'd handed him the ring that he was too shocked to take. She'd had to place it in his hand and fold his fingers over it.

I just can't do this, Leo.

And now he was taking on even more responsibility, re-sponsibility that would require a greater commitment. Once he signed these papers, he was locked into restaurant life, something Carol Ann had never been able to get used to. She'd resented how much time he'd spent helping his father at the Franklin location. And what about Mandy? Would he ever have time to get to know her now? Would this be the end of their fledgling relationship?

"All right, Leonardo, it's your turn," their attorney said. "The next generation of Romanos takes over."

Leo sat up and reached for his father's pen.

Father God, please help me do this.

Wednesday afternoon, Mandy sat at her home desk and twirled her hair around her finger, staring at the blank screen on her computer. She hated writing bad reviews. *Hated* it. But sometimes she just couldn't find a way around it. She started typing:

The Steak Shack's fifties decor is fun and…

And my cheeseburger was undercooked. The waitress serving me obviously hates her life. My chocolate milkshake was watery. The bathroom needed to be cleaned. Etcetera, etcetera, etcetera!

Mandy shut her laptop fiercely, deciding to work on her column when she wasn't so distracted. She checked her watch again. In two hours, she was meeting Leo for their third try at a date. And this time, she was determined to at least refrain from calling him a liar and walking out. She took special care with her hair and makeup. Ashley called several times, offering suggestions for what Mandy should wear, how she should act and what she should say. While her advice could be trying, talking to Ashley helped Mandy feel less nervous.

At ten to seven, Mandy walked through the door of El Camino Blanco, her favorite Mexican restaurant in the heart of Denver.

The hostess smiled at her. "Miss Seymour, your table is ready. We're so glad to have you tonight."

"Thank you, Amelia. Did Javier tell you—"

"Oh, yes. Don't worry. We've got your favorite table ready for you."

"Mandy?"

Mandy turned at the sound of Leo's voice. She couldn't stop the smile that came to her face. His dark hair framed his face and his loose, black shirt looked great against his olive complexion. And the lack of tension and anger between them already made this meeting a hundred times better than their previous encounter.

"Hi, Leo," she said, hoping he didn't notice the quaver in her voice.

"Follow me," Amelia said.

"Have you ever been here before?" Mandy asked. Leo shook his head.

"I thought I knew all the good places in Denver, but I think you probably have me beat on that."

As Mandy slid into the booth across from Leo, she shrugged. "I sort of have an advantage, I guess, when it comes to knowing about all the good places to eat."

Leo looked at the surrounding area. "This is an interesting restaurant."

Mandy nodded, not mentioning that she'd called ahead and asked the owner, Javier, for a favor, which he was happy to oblige since Mandy had written several starred reviews for him.

El Camino Blanco was a tiny restaurant. The walls were covered with sombreros, Mexican flags and paintings created by Javier's wife. The booth tucked away in the corner where Mandy and Leo were seated was the best seat in the house; it offered privacy in an otherwise crowded space.

Their waiter, Victor, whom Mandy also knew by name, came to the table, balancing water and two plates on his tray. He set a pitcher of water between them and a covered dish of warm, freshly made flour tortillas, along with a dish of melted butter.

"Nice to see you, Miss Seymour. Your meal should be ready momentarily."

Leo looked across the table in surprise.

"I hope you don't mind, but I ordered ahead for us."

"Not at all. I trust your judgment."

Mandy tore a tortilla in half and dipped it into the butter. "Try this. You'll love it."

Leo did the same, a slow smile creeping onto his face. "I think I could eat a dozen of these tortillas by myself."

Mandy shook her head. "Oh, no, Mr. Romano. You have to share with me."

He caught her gaze and held it. Mandy cleared her throat nervously and tore another tortilla in half.

"So tell me—why another Romano's?" Mandy asked. Leo was quiet for several moments before answering.

"It's my father's gift to me, I guess you could say."

Mandy looked up with interest. "Really?"

"And it's my gift to him."

Now Mandy was really interested. "How so?"

Leo looked at her seriously. "This conversation is between us alone, correct? Nothing would ever end up in one of your columns?"

Mandy chose not to be offended by that insinuation. "Of course not."

He nodded. "My father has Parkinson's disease. This is something that he's been struggling with for a while, but the effects were minimal for a long time and didn't interfere much with his daily life. However, over the past few months, the symptoms have started progressing. He's still in relatively good health, but it's clear this path is one that will get worse over time. And it's obvious he needs to make adjustments to his schedule and lifestyle in order to stay as healthy as he can for as long as he can.

"Having said that, I think my dad has always wanted me to have a restaurant of my own—one that would reflect my tastes and preferences. But it was never seriously discussed until several months ago. My dad's suggestion to open another Romano's came at a time when I was feeling a bit lost. I had been engaged, and the engagement ended. My father thought it would help…distract me, I guess. He wanted us to do this endeavor together. It was important to him. So we did."

"It was important to him," Mandy repeated. "And you?" she asked. The conflicted look in Leo's expression didn't escape her.

"To me, too. For different reasons, but it was and is important to me. Cooking has been my passion for a long time. Going to culinary school was my choice. I knew I wanted to cook as my profession—but I guess I never really hoped to own my own restaurant. All my life, I've seen how much responsibility that was for my father. I would be content just running a kitchen without the added stress of ownership.

"Anyway, that's not how things have ended up. I've taken over the Franklin Romano's. I actually signed the paperwork this morning, making it official. I'm already looking for a head chef for my Romano's."

Mandy inhaled sharply. "You're running the Franklin Romano's? Your father is—"

"*Has* retired. It's time. His health can't take the stress of running the restaurants. He hasn't been cooking for a long time, of course. He has very capable staff to run his kitchens. But the administrative side of running a restaurant is even more stressful than managing a kitchen. He can't do it any longer."

"That's going to be a lot of stress on you now, I imagine," Mandy said, wishing she could reach over and touch Leo's hand.

He took a sip of water. Mandy watched as the condensation ran down the glass.

"With God's help, I can do it," he responded.

Victor returned at that moment, followed by another waiter, both holding trays filled with food. Fiery, mouth-watering smells filled the air around them.

"We have the seafood enchiladas wrapped in blue corn tortillas with refried beans and rice, the chicken tostadas with black-bean-and-corn salsa and the pork tamales with green chili."

The waiter set the platters between them and left two plates so they could share the dishes. Mandy asked if Leo would mind if she prayed before they ate. Her simple yet sincere prayer calmed the anxiety in Leo. She finished the prayer and reached for the platter of enchiladas. For a moment Leo just watched her, knowing he didn't want that to be the last time he ever heard Mandy Seymour pray. He wanted to share more meals with her. He wanted to hear her pray, and to talk with her as they were now, quietly over dinner.

The thought took him by surprise.

Leo took a bite of tamale and enjoyed the spicy taste slowly.

"I can tell this is going to be a meal to remember. Promise me, Mandy, that you'll take me to all of your favorite restaurants."

Mandy lifted a tostada to her lips. "We'll see. I've got a lot of favorites."

Half an hour later, Leo leaned back, feeling so full he had no idea how he could eat another bite. But when their waiter placed a dish with warm sopaipillas and honey on the table, he couldn't help himself. He followed Mandy's lead and dipped a corner of a sopaipilla into the honey.

"This is incredible," he said and Mandy nodded.

"This was the first restaurant I ever wrote a review for."

Leo looked at her in surprise. "Really? When was that?"

Mandy looked past him, scanning the small restaurant. "A few years ago. It was so easy to write the review. I loved everything they served me, and have ever since. I've tried everything on the menu. Javier, the owner, is an amazing cook. He immigrated to Denver from Mexico when he was nineteen, alone, without his family. He started this restaurant when he was just twenty-one years old."

Leo leaned forward. He liked the faraway look in Mandy's eyes as she told Javier's story.

"What made you become a food critic, Mandy?" he asked. She laughed nervously and he could see the discomfiture on her face.

"I love food. Can't you tell?"

He frowned. He hadn't wanted to make her feel embarrassed.

"So do I."

She stirred her cup of coffee. "It's different for you."

"What do you mean?" he asked. But she just shook her head.

"It just is. Next question."

Leo decided not to press the issue. Not yet, anyway. "All right. Where did this love of food come from?"

Mandy stared down at the table. "My mother, I guess. Though she'd probably hate it if she knew I'd said that." Mandy was obviously uncomfortable with the subject, but Leo wasn't quite ready to move on.

"Explain that to me," he said gently.

After a moment, she sighed and started talking. "My mother is a talented cook. She can make the most delicious meals out of anything. She'd whip up a gourmet meal out of whatever we had in the pantry when I was growing up. She's also a perfectionist, which means her expectations for her children are extremely high. I was expected to be a certain weight, which I exceeded. I was expected to be a certain height, which I never reached. I was expected to marry someone right out of college. Unfortunately, no one asked me. I was expected to live out her dreams, none of which included writing a column about food and living alone."

Leo didn't like the flat, despondent tone Mandy's voice had shifted to while talking about her mother. The bright, excited look in her eyes she'd had as they'd shared dinner and laughed back and forth vanished as she talked about falling beneath her mother's expectations.

"What were her dreams?" Leo wondered. Mandy looked confused.

"What do you mean?"

"Your mother's dreams for herself—what were they?"

Mandy was thoughtful. "That's a really good question. And I can't believe it, but I haven't really thought about it before. I know she always wanted to travel. But she and my dad never did—I don't really know why. I'm sure they could have afforded to. My dad's a whiz with budgets and he loves making plans and budgeting and saving for things."

She paused for a moment and sighed. "I think she wanted a more glamorous life than the one she ended up living. My dad loves small-town life. And my mom loves him, so they settled in Evergreen. I think she wanted a big, grand house where she could host dinner parties. They have a beautiful home, but it's older and sort of rustic. And she never hosted any grand parties.

"My mom was one of those really beautiful, popular girls when she was in high school. She was homecoming queen and all that. And in college, she always had lots of friends. She was the girl all the boys noticed. Getting older seems to be difficult for her, though I think she's still very beautiful. But she equates beauty with youth. She also equates it with being thin. I'm not thin enough for her. And I've always looked more like my dad—I've got brown hair like him, while my mother has blond hair. I've got brown eyes—she's got blue eyes. I've got freckles—she's got a perfect complexion. She married young. I loved college and ended up getting my master's in creative writing. She had children young. I'm, obviously, not at that place in my life yet. I'm just an all-around failure in her eyes."

Leo winced at the pain lacing that statement.

"You're not a failure, Mandy," he told her. She placed her napkin on the table and shrugged, keeping her gaze on the tablecloth.

"No, I'm not. But when I look at her, I can see that's what she's thinking. And it's not easy to be a failure in your parent's eyes."

Leo nodded with complete understanding. "I know. I've been trying to avoid that my whole life."

"And succeeding, I would imagine," Mandy said, but her

voice held no malice. Leo wished he could somehow erase the hurt in her countenance.

"Mandy, I…"

"If you don't mind my asking, what happened with your engagement?" she asked.

Leo's mouth tightened. She couldn't know, of course, that talking about it never seemed to help. That he always felt worse afterward.

Still, he figured that Mandy was entitled to know at least some of the details—after everything she'd just shared with him

"Well, my fiancée, Carol Ann, and I had dated since our senior year of college. After college she got her master's in business and spent a few months abroad. She had a lot of goals for herself. We stayed together through all of this. There had never been any doubt, in my mind, anyway, that we would get married. She said yes when I asked her. But six months later she told me that she couldn't marry me, that she could see our future stretching out in front of her and it wasn't what she wanted. She took her freedom and left me with a broken heart."

"Oh, Leo," Mandy whispered. "That's terrible."

"It certainly wasn't what I would have chosen. But I know it would have been worse for her to have married me and buried those feelings. She wouldn't have been happy, and I wouldn't have been happy when those true feelings surfaced. The problem was—I *thought* we were happy. I wanted to marry her more than anything."

Leo felt that he was rambling and needed to stop.

What are you doing? Crying to her about how badly you wanted to marry another woman? What's wrong with you?

They stopped talking as their waiter came by and re-filled their cups of coffee. Leo watched as Mandy care-fully poured a spoonful of cream into her cup, and then two packets of sweetener. He smiled. It was obviously a system that worked for her. He'd have to remember that: one cream, two sweeteners.

He blinked at the realization that he was thinking ahead, already planning to see her again.

The thought of Carol Ann leaving him still shocked and confused him—he'd thought they had a great relationship. He couldn't go through that again. And with that thought, Leo pulled back and began to argue with himself.

Slow down. You like her but you hardly know her. You thought you knew Carol Ann and look where that got you.

He glanced down at his watch. "It's nearly closing time!"

Mandy looked surprised. "Really? I didn't realize it was so late. I was so caught up in our conversation that I…" Her voice trailed off and she just cocked her head and smiled at him. That smile—hopeful but cautious—made Leo want to keep drinking coffee and talking to her over shared sopaipillas. But it was late, and he worried he'd already shared too much.

"I've had a great time, too, Mandy. So, third time's the charm they say, right?"

She laughed out loud and Leo bit his lip, trying not to think about how much he liked the musical sound of her laugh.

"I think it just might be true in our case," she said. Leo motioned for their waiter to come over as he signed the credit card receipt.

"I hope everything was to your liking, Miss Seymour," the waiter said, taking the receipt.

"Delicious as usual, Victor. Tell Javier he outdid himself this time."

Leo walked Mandy to her car, wondering what she expected of him at that moment. Surely she didn't want him to kiss her…or did she? He felt more than out of practice when it came to dating etiquette.

Lucky for him, Mandy didn't seem as anxiety ridden.

She took out her keys and unlocked her car door, then looked up at him with a warm smile.

"This was so nice, Leo. I'd love to do it again sometime. But I know you have a lot going on with the restaurants right now. Why don't you just call me when you might be available to go out again. If you want to, I mean!"

Leo wanted to laugh at Mandy's outburst. She'd obviously tacked on that last line as an afterthought and her cheeks flushed with embarrassment.

But he didn't laugh. "Thanks for understanding, Mandy. And yes, I will definitely call you."

"Next time, the restaurant is your choice," Mandy said, a slight tremor in her voice.

Leo had absolutely no idea what to do at that moment. She probably didn't realize how that little tremor in her voice captivated him. They stood there awkwardly with Leo feeling like a fish out of water. So he did the first thing that came to him.

"Until next time then, Mandy." He took her hand and kissed it.

Chapter 7

"Did you just tell me that this guy kissed your hand!?"

Mandy giggled at the shriek in Ashley's voice. The two girls were seated side by side at Starbucks. Mandy had just a few minutes until she had to leave for work, but Ashley had insisted on meeting in person for a rundown of Mandy's date.

"Shh! Not so loud, Ashley. And yes, he kissed my hand. It was romantic and charming...and perfect."

"Did you swoon?"

"People don't swoon anymore, Ashley. People don't even know what that word means."

"It means—"

"I know what it means!"

"So...did ya?"

Mandy elbowed her. "Maybe a little, once I was in my car."

Ashley burst out laughing.

Mandy thought again of dinner with Leo—the laughter, the food, the way he watched her so intently. It was quite possibly the best date of her life.

Thursday evening Leo drove as fast as he could to University of Colorado Hospital, listening to Isa talk on speaker phone.

"Dad is annoyed that we brought him in. Mom is wringing her hands with worry, and I'm going nuts trying to calm them both down. How far away are you?" Isa's tone was calm but Leo knew she was concerned. As a nightshift E.R. nurse, Isa was comfortable in hospitals and probably the member of the family who best understood her father's disease, but still, Leo knew seeing their dad so vulnerable was hard for her, too.

"I'll be there in fifteen minutes. Maybe a little more. What about you? Are you scheduled to work tonight?"

"Yes, but I can be late. I'm not going anywhere until you're here. What about the restaurants?"

"They can survive without me."

"Okay, well, from what I can tell, they're going to release Dad. I— Oh, here comes the doctor now, Leo. I need to talk to her. See you soon."

The line clicked off and Leo gripped the steering wheel. He slowed his speed just a tad, relieved that Isa was with their parents and speaking to the doctor.

As he pulled into the parking lot and ran into the building, Isa texted him the room number.

So they are admitting Dad. This can't be good.

He rushed around the corner and saw his mother and Isa arguing in the hallway.

"Ah, Leonardo," his mother said. "Tell your sister that I am most certainly staying overnight with your father."

Isa gave an exasperated huff.

"Mom, you should really go home and rest and come back early tomorrow. I can stay with Dad," Leo offered.

His mother clucked her tongue and shook her head. "And what of the restaurants? No, you go and I will stay."

"The restaurants are fine. My staff is perfectly capable of handling things without me for one night. I can stay. You won't get any sleep on that small uncomfortable cot."

"Dad wants you to go home, Mom," Isa said. "I can pick

you up first thing in the morning and we'll come back together."

His mother frowned but finally nodded. After they all
filed into the room and his mother had hugged and kissed
their father and tried to insist one last time that she stay
overnight, Leo and Isa stepped aside and Isa hurriedly re-
layed to him what had happened.

"He stood up and his blood pressure dropped dramati-
cally, so he fainted, taking a table down with him. This
kind of thing—low blood pressure—isn't uncommon for
people with Parkinson's, Leo. He cut his arm on the table.
Mom was terrified and called me. When I got there, he
was having trouble getting up. He was awake but groggy.
I managed to get him on the sofa and wrap his arm, but
we needed help so I called an ambulance. We brought him
here and Dr. Rosas saw him and said she wants to adjust
his medication and watch him overnight. He had to have
just a few stitches."

Leo bit his lower lip. Isa reached out and touched his
shoulder.

"It's okay, Leo. These things happen. We'll get his meds
where they need to be and we'll move on. He's going to be
okay."

"This time," Leo pointed out.

Isa remained unflustered. "That's all we can do. We have
to take this one step at a time. I'll drive Mom home. You
go stay with Dad. He's hungry so order him some food and
try to encourage him. You know how frustrating these epi-
sodes are for him. He hates feeling so dependent on others."

Leo nodded. "I need to call the restaurants and check in."

"Do that. I'll take Mom home. And call me if anything
changes. *Anything*." Isa hugged Leo tightly. "Trust me,
Leo. Let's just concentrate on helping Mom and Dad get
through this."

Leo sighed and hugged her back, knowing she was right.
He walked farther down the hallway, pulled out his cell

phone and called both Jeremy and Adam to let them know he couldn't come in. It was a Sunday night and he knew both places would be packed, but Leo trusted Jeremy and Adam to handle things as though he were there. Still, the worry of the restaurants hung over him as he walked into his father's room.

Sitting up in the hospital bed, Leo's dad seemed to be trying to figure out how to work the remote control. Leo walked over to him. "Let me have that thing, Dad. I'm sure I can find us an old Clint Eastwood movie or something." His dad's hand shook badly as he held out the remote control. Leo took the remote, sat down on the edge of the bed and looked straight into his father's eyes.

"Are you okay?" he asked. He could see the frustration, anger, helplessness—every emotion that he felt, as well—all over his dad's face. His father closed his eyes.

"I don't want this to be happening to me. I don't want this," Gabriel Romano, the man Leo respected and loved more than anyone else on earth, stared down at his shaking hands and drew in a raspy breath.

"I don't want this for you, either. I'm so sorry, Dad. It's not fair."

His dad looked back up at him. "No, it's not fair. That's okay."

But Leo shook his head. "It's *not* okay. *This is not okay.*" he couldn't keep his voice from rising or the emotion from filling his words.

"Son, listen to me."

Leo didn't want to hear his dad try to convince him that this was God's will. That good would come out of this. He didn't want to hear any of it. But what could he do at that moment? Leave? Argue with his father? Leo gritted his teeth and prepared to hear the platitudes he'd heard all his life. He would listen and be respectful. He didn't necessarily have to agree.

"I'd rather be grateful for the incredible life I've lived,

than bitter and angry over things that I can't control. Everyone knows that life isn't fair. But here's what I have—a wife who has been the love of my life, a brilliant daughter who has so much strength and a son who is by my side and will be until the end. That's more than I could have asked for."

Leo took his dad's hand in his, his heart heavy with hurt. "You're right. I'll be with you every step of the way. Good days and bad."

"I know," Gabriel said. "And I have a faith that sustains me when I need it most. Your faith can do the same, Leo. I know you're struggling right now. I know this is hard for you."

Leo didn't respond.

Later that night, after they'd shared an early meal, Gabriel fell asleep as they watched an old Western on TV. As his father snored softly, Leo lay awake on the cot, listening to the heart monitor beeping and thinking about what his dad had said about things he couldn't control and life being unfair. Those thoughts inevitably made him think of Carol Ann.

The fear and concern for his father outweighed the anger and bitterness he felt toward Carol Ann. Still, Leo wondered if those feelings regarding Carol Ann were really subsiding, even apart from the distraction of his father's illness. He wanted what his father had: a devoted wife who loved him with every breath. Children who were committed to their family. A happy home. If Carol Ann couldn't give him those things—he no longer wanted a life with her.

It was time to move on.

He thought of Mandy.

"Where are you again?" Mandy asked. She'd been thrilled that Leo had called so soon after their date, then sad to hear that his father was in the hospital.

"I'm on my way to the Franklin restaurant," Leo told her. "My dad is home and I've got a million things to do— payroll, dinner prep. I'm cooking tonight."

Mandy could hear the strain in his voice.

"Is there anything I can do?" she asked.

"No, but thank you for asking, Mandy. I just wanted to say how much I enjoyed our date."

Mandy smiled. "Me, too. I'll be praying for your dad, Leo."

Ten minutes later, Mandy was rushing through the parking lot to reach her car. She glanced upward, knowing that the cloud-covered sky mixed with freezing temperatures was a recipe for a snowstorm. And she fully intended to be home by the time that storm hit. Once she pulled out onto the freeway, her cell buzzed and she pushed the speaker button.

"Mandy, it's Brian."

"Brian! Hey, what's up?"

"Is there any chance you can come out to Evergreen?"

Mandy's heart jumped into her throat. "What's happened? Are Mom and Dad okay? What about Samantha?"

"Everyone's okay, but unfortunately, Mom slipped on ice out on the deck this afternoon and has some pretty painful bruises on her back and tailbone. She's going to need to take it easy for a few days. And even more unfortunate, Dad had to fly to Dallas today for a business deal. He'll be back Tuesday. If you could come out for the weekend, that would be great. Sam would go stay with her but she has a really bad cold right now and there's no way she has the energy to deal with Mom. I can only go over there so often while Sam's sick."

"Of course I'll come," Mandy said, but even as the words left her mouth, snow started coming down fast, powdering her windshield. If she took the time to go to her apartment, the roads might be too bad to make it to Evergreen. "I'm on my way," Mandy said before hanging up, switching lanes and leaving for Evergreen.

An hour and a half later, she pulled into her parents'

driveway, glad she'd made the decision to head straight over. Traffic had been heavy and visibility became worse the closer she got to Evergreen. Brian opened the front door and she stepped inside the warm house. Mandy stopped for a moment to compose herself. The sound of crackling wood and the smell of her mother's favorite vanilla-scented candles were so familiar to her.

"You built a fire?" she asked Brian.

"Mom insisted. She's drinking tea and resting on the living room sofa. Can you make dinner?"

Mandy pushed him toward the door. "You know I can. You get back to Samantha. We'll be fine here."

Brian looked skeptical.

"Go!" Mandy insisted and Brian nodded before ducking out of the house.

"Amanda, is that you?" her mother called out.

Here we go.

Mandy took off her coat and made her way to the living room. "I'm here, Mom. How are you feeling?"

Her mother pulled the afghan on her lap closer to her chin. "Absolutely terrible. I can't believe I fell down. My back will be black-and-blue tomorrow. Your father has called every ten minutes, worried as can be. He hadn't been gone an hour before I slipped out on the deck. It's so icy out there. I was planning to bring in a few sticks of firewood—you know how I love a roaring fire when it snows—when splat! I'm on the ground."

"It happens to everybody, Mom."

"It happens to old people, which I guess I am."

Mandy rolled her eyes. "Fifty-five is not old, Mom! You know what people say—you're only as old as you feel."

"Perfect. I feel like I'm ninety right now."

"I fell down just last week," Mandy told her. Her mother gave her a very familiar look.

"Yes, but that's *you,* Mandy."

"What does that mean?"

Her mother closed her eyes. "Never mind. I need more painkiller. And are you going to cook?"

"Sure. What do you want me to make?"

"Oh, it doesn't matter. I'm not that hungry. See what you can find in the cupboard."

Mandy ran her fingers over the kitchen island, humming as she opened the cupboard and inspected what there was to eat. The kitchen had always been her favorite room in the house. Her father had specially designed it for her mother. The large kitchen island was surrounded by plenty of cabinets and counter space. A round antique table sat in front of large bay windows, the same place where she and Brian had had breakfast every morning before school.

The thought of breakfast gave her an idea. Mandy set out a container of cinnamon and the canister of sugar and turned up the heat on the stove before pulling out a carton of eggs and getting to work.

Thirty minutes later she brought her mother a tray with a stack of warm French toast, complete with powdered sugar and a jar of maple syrup.

"French toast!" her mother exclaimed in surprise.

"It sounded good to me," Mandy said, curling up on the easy chair across from her mom, her plate in her lap, a tall glass of milk on the side table. She knew that French toast was one of her mother's favorite breakfast dishes.

"Did you put a little flour in the eggs?" her mother asked.

"Of course I did, Mom. Who do you think taught me how to make French toast?"

Mandy could see her mom trying to hide a smile. When her cell phone buzzed, Mandy reached for her phone and froze when she saw Leo's name come up.

Having a conversation with Leo while Mom's within ear-shot is not happening.

Mandy silenced her phone and settled back into the easy chair.

"Who was that?" her mother asked.

"Just a friend," Mandy answered.

"Well, fine. You don't have to tell me," her mother huffed. Mandy tried not to roll her eyes. At least, not where her mother could see.

"Okay, his name is Leo and he's a new friend of mine."

"Leo? Is that Spanish?"

"Italian. His family's from Italy. He actually owns an Italian restaurant in Denver."

"Well, then, he's perfect for you."

Mandy felt her throat constrict.

Of course. Because I love to eat so much. It only makes sense that a girl who wears a size ten should end up with a cook.

"Mom, what do you mean by that?"

"Oh, Mandy, stop analyzing everything," her mother waved her off. "Take this to the kitchen, please."

Mandy felt tears burning in her eyes but she stubbornly held them off. She took both of their dishes to the kitchen and spent the next twenty minutes loading the dishwasher and wiping down the counters. When she felt slightly more in control of her emotions, she returned to the living room with a glass of water and more pain reliever for her mother.

"Can I get you anything else? Do you want me to help you to your bed?" Mandy asked.

Her mother shook her head. "Not yet. I was just thinking…you know this reminds me of when you and Brian had chicken pox at the same time."

Mandy sat back down. "Why?"

"Because I made you French toast. I remember that Brian kept scratching, even though I told him not to. But you didn't scratch. And when I asked you what you wanted to eat, you said French toast."

Mandy leaned her head back on the chair. "I remember. You took such good care of us."

Her mother smoothed the blanket over her. "And here you are, taking care of me. Making me French toast."

Mandy hoped this wasn't about to segue into another example of how her mother felt old.

"That's what families do for each other, I guess," Mandy said.

"So tell me about Leo," her mother said. Mandy didn't want to. She really didn't want to. But she also didn't want to ruin this somewhat peaceful moment with her mother.

"Well, like I said, he owns a restaurant. He's nice. He's handsome. I think we're about the same age. He…has a lot of family responsibilities."

"Like what?" her mother pressed. Mandy didn't want to overshare what Leo had asked her to keep private.

"His father is a well-known chef, as well, and owns a successful restaurant in Denver, too. Anyway, the restaurant business is very demanding and Leo helps his dad a lot. He's a hard worker. His faith is important to him. His family is everything to him."

"You really like him, don't you?" her mother asked.

Mandy hesitated. Sharing things with her mother usually ended badly for her—with her mom bringing things back up at the worst moments.

"I'm just interested in knowing him better. But I like what I've seen so far."

"He sounds like a very successful young man."

Mandy thought about the stress so evident in Leo's eyes. "He is. But he works hard for it."

Neither of them spoke for a full minute. Her mother's eyes stayed downward toward the blanket as she finally said, "You know, when I was younger, I wanted to go to culinary school."

Is Mom actually sharing something about herself with me? I think I've entered the Twilight Zone.

"You never told me that," Mandy said softly.

Her mom shrugged. "It was just a crazy notion I had for a while. I never did anything about it. I suppose I wanted to be Julia Child and learn to cook in Paris."

Mandy and her mom both chuckled.

"What else?" Mandy pressed. Her mom blinked and looked over at her.

"What else?"

"What else did you dream about, Mom?"

Her mom looked at the burning and crackling fire.

"Well, I always wanted to stand right below the big Christmas tree at Rockefeller Center in New York. Silly, I know."

Mandy shook her head. "I don't think that's silly. I think that sounds wonderful. What else?"

"Oh, lots of things. I wanted romance and adventure, moments where I felt completely alive. I wanted to see a whale out in the ocean."

Mandy smiled.

"And I wanted to have just one moment where I truly felt God's favor over me."

Mandy swallowed the lump in her throat. She couldn't believe that her mom would share that with her.

"Don't misunderstand. I've felt close to God, I've felt Him with me at some of my darkest moments and some of my happiest. But I don't think I've ever felt His favor over me."

"Me, either. But I want to," Mandy said, her words just above a whisper.

Her mom looked over at her. "What are your dreams, Mandy?"

The tears that she had held back earlier came forward

without warning. Mandy laughed at herself awkwardly and wiped her eyes.

"What's wrong?" her mom asked, her voice filled with concern.

"Nothing."

"Tell me, Amanda."

Mandy sniffed and tried not to let any more tears escape. "It's just…that's the first time you've ever asked me that, Mom."

Her mom looked down at her hands and didn't respond. Mandy tried to push past the unease of the moment.

"But since you have now, I'll tell you. I dream of feeling comfortable in my own skin. I dream of being a renowned food columnist. I dream of marrying someone who will love me like Dad loves you. I dream of having a daughter of my own one day. I'll tell her that she's beautiful, that she's loved, that she's everything. I dream of having a house that I can decorate just the way I want. And you know what else?" Mandy said. Her mom lifted her gaze to meet Mandy's.

"I have *always* wanted to see a whale in the ocean."

Her mom laughed loudly. "Are you serious?"

Mandy nodded and laughed with her. Once the laughter ceased, Mandy braved one more question.

"Mom, when did you give up on your dreams?"

Her mother closed her eyes. "I don't know. It just happened. I grew up. Romance and adventure aren't exactly priorities when you're busy paying a mortgage and raising children and cooking for the church potluck. Life happens and other things become more important. Baseball games and spelling bees and chickenpox—life was busy."

"But it was never enough, was it?" Mandy wondered.

Her mom's gaze went back to the fire. Mandy could see the rigidness in her neck. "Looking back—maybe not. In some ways, I think I lost myself along the way. Or I became someone else. There were so many things I'd wanted to do,

and time went by so fast. I never accomplished anything."
Her mother's words were flat and lifeless.

"How can you say that? You accomplished so many
things! You've been married for thirty years. You raised
two children. Are Brian and I really such a disappointment
to you?" Mandy asked, her voice rising. Her mom faced
her, looking surprised.

"Of course not. I'm not disappointed in you."

Mandy stood up, unable to stay calm. "Yes, you are!
Brian should already have been promoted at work. Brian
and Samantha should have had a baby by now. Sound familiar? I'm a size ten instead of a size six. I have a career
but no husband or children of my own. I'm nothing special."

"Mandy, stop!" her mother shouted over Mandy's rant.
Mandy's mouth zipped shut. Her chest heaved and tears
streamed down her face. Her mother's eyes were wide in
shock.

"Do you realize how you make me feel? Like I'm not
good enough. Like I'm a failure!" Mandy cried before sitting
back onto the chair and covering her face with her hands.
For several moments the only sounds in the room were of
embers popping and Mandy sniffing because her nose was
running like a faucet.

"Mandy, I'm the failure. Not you," her mother said, her
words so quiet they were almost inaudible. She wiped her
eyes. "Or I've *felt* like a failure. I have a college degree,
but I never had a career. I took care of my husband and
my children and while that was my priority and it was a
good one—I had dreams for myself beyond that. I look at
you—and I see a young, independent woman who has made
a name for herself and who is capable of so many things.
And you have so much life stretched out before you. So
much time."

Mandy looked up, taking a moment to find her courage.
"Mom, when I look at you, I see a woman with a perfect op-

portunity to be happy, but she lives in a state of discontent-ment. I'm at a place in my life where I'm working to support myself. Life doesn't seem to slow down for me. And I'm not where I thought I'd be at this age. But for you— Dad will retire next year. You've made wise financial decisions, and you live in a home that's paid off. You have the means to travel and experience wonderful things. There are no parenting responsibilities to hold you back anymore. You can do whatever you want. Plan a trip and go whale watch-ing. Sign up for a cooking class at the community college."

Mandy took a shaky breath. "Because of your example, I struggle to be contented with my own life. And I don't want that. I don't want to always wish I were thinner, to always wish I had a different life, to always be looking for something else. This is me, this is who I am." Mandy mo-tioned to her body.

"I don't think it's going to get better than this. I'm never going to be beautiful like you. I might not ever be a wife and mother." At that moment, Mandy had to steady herself because the words hurt to even speak. "But I think I still have value as a person. And I want to live feeling valued, not inferior. I can't live that way, Mom!" Mandy cried out as another wave of tears rolled down her face.

Her mother leaned over on the sofa and wept. After a few moments, both women crying, Mandy stood up and walked toward the staircase.

"Mandy, wait," her mother said finally. Mandy stopped, her hand on the stair railing, and turned around to look at her mom.

Amid her tears, her mother said the words that Mandy never thought she'd hear:

"I'm sorry."

Mandy stood, frozen, transfixed by those two simple words.

"I'm sorry, Mandy," her mother repeated.

Mandy somehow knew that the unfamiliar feeling that was stirring inside of her was her heart...perhaps finally beginning to heal.

Chapter 8

Leo inspected the produce that filled the kitchen counters—squeezing a tomato to see if it was ripe, smelling a zucchini to ensure it was fresh—all while listening to the banter and joking of his staff throughout the kitchen as they prepped for the dinner rush.

"So the date last Wednesday was a success, huh?" Angelina winked at him as she set another crate of lettuce on the counter. Leo had asked her to work at the Franklin restaurant for the past few days to help cover some short-staffed shifts. He'd expected to be interrogated about the date as soon as Angelina saw him again.

Leo grabbed his clipboard to scan the specials menu for that evening and gave Angelina a slight nod.

"Yes, it went well. I hope to see her again."

"Good. I liked her."

"Me, too," Leo responded as he opened the freezer to look over what they had, checking off items on his list. "Angelina," he called from the freezer. "We need more provolone. I didn't realize we were so low."

"Got it. I'll make sure we have more for tonight. You know, chef—" Angelina poked her head into the freezer "—you should invite her to dinner with the family."

Leo laughed. "I don't want to scare her off."

Angelina punched his shoulder. "We're a lovable bunch and you know it. Invite her!"

Leo left his Romano's and drove to the sister restaurant, considering Angelina's idea to invite Mandy to dinner. Once a month, his family had a large potluck dinner together, usually at his parents' home. It had always been his dad's favorite time to try out new recipes. Family dinner was next Monday.

Maybe I should invite her.

Leo had tried to keep Mandy at a respectable distance from his thoughts ever since their date, but that had proved to be impossible. He kept thinking about the way she laughed, the gold flecks in her brown eyes, the way she closed her eyes when she tasted something delicious and then insisted Leo try it, as well.

The way her hand had smelled like honey when he'd kissed it.

They'd spoken only for a few short minutes when she'd returned his call Friday night, enough time for Mandy to explain that her mother had hurt her back and Mandy would be staying with her in Evergreen for a few days.

A few days felt too long. It was Monday and he'd wanted to call her every day, but he didn't want to seem so eager. Then again, maybe she wanted him to call. Maybe the longer he waited to call, the more worried she'd be that he wasn't interested in pursuing her.

Leo sighed in frustration. As he locked the car door and walked through the kitchen entrance of the Franklin restaurant, an idea formed in his head. He left the staff in the kitchen and wandered into his father's office. Leo stopped in the center of the office and looked around. He hadn't changed a thing since taking over the restaurant.

Maybe it's time for me to make some changes.

But first, Leo sat down and dialed Mandy's number on his cell phone.

"Mandy, it's Leo."

"Leo." The fact that he could almost hear her smile as she said his name brought an automatic smile to his own face.

"I was thinking—since you're in Evergreen with your mother, well, I was wondering if I could…" His words stuck in his throat and he coughed.

"Leo, just tell me," Mandy said in that calm way of hers that he appreciated.

"I'd love to come up and cook dinner for you and your mother one evening."

Mandy didn't answer for a moment and Leo's brow began to sweat.

It was a stupid idea. I'm basically inviting myself over. Her mom is hurt, the last thing she needs is a stranger coming to her home.

"You would do that?"

Mandy's astonishment made Leo pause.

"Of course. When would work for you?"

"Tonight?" she asked. The hopeful tone in Mandy's voice stirred feelings in Leo that he hadn't felt in years. Like the excitement of a teenager going on his first date. All those emotions—caused by one word.

I'm in trouble.

Leo glanced at his staff sheet to see who was coming in that evening. It was a strong lineup, but he felt uncertain. He wasn't scheduled to cook, but he felt an obligation to be at one of the restaurants.

Dating just doesn't work very well with a chef's schedule.

Still, Leo wanted to see Mandy so badly that he decided he'd just have to make it work.

"Tonight. Six o'clock all right?"

"Perfect. See you then."

Mandy set her phone down on the nightstand by her old bed in her parents' house and then sank onto the bed.

Leonardo Romano wanted to drive to tiny old Evergreen, Colorado, just to cook dinner for Mandy and her mother.

That thought left flutters in her stomach. Within twenty seconds, the smile slipped from her face as she thought about her mother meeting Leo. Mandy tossed around the idea of just surprising her mother, not telling her that Leo would be joining them for dinner, or more accurately, he'd be their personal chef for the evening.

But she knew that a surprise like that could start a world war.

With a dejected huff, Mandy went downstairs to tell her the news.

Ten minutes later, she'd already told her twice and yet her mother still sat on the sofa with a confused look on her face.

"So he's coming here?"

Mandy nodded with a patience that could only have been divinely bestowed on her at that moment.

"Yes, Mom. Leo's coming over to cook dinner for us tonight."

"I thought he had restaurants to run."

"He does. But he also has staff to run his kitchens. He doesn't have to be there every minute."

"Why is he coming here?"

Mandy's opened her mouth to answer, but then closed it again.

Good question.

"He wants to, I guess."

"Well, you'd better help me into the bathtub. I need to wash my hair. You'll have to style it for me."

Mandy pursed her lips to keep from saying, *Yes, Mom. Because it's all about you. I'm the single gal here, remember? But let's make sure your hair is styled to perfection.*

Mandy kept her comments to herself, unwilling to start even the slightest squabble with her mother. She spent the next few hours cleaning her parents' kitchen from top to bottom in preparation for *the* Leonardo Romano to use it. She set the table with her mother's good china, and then, as ordered, she helped her mother get ready for their special guest.

Finally, Mandy dashed upstairs and took a lightning-fast shower and threw on her jeans with the same brown sweater she'd worn to work on Friday. Since she'd left for Evergreen without stopping by her apartment, her choices were limited. She rushed downstairs, lighting candles and finding a Frank Sinatra CD to play on her parents' stereo. When her mother saw her, Claire simply raised her eyebrows and said, "Aren't you going to wear some jewelry to liven up that outfit? If you didn't bring anything with you, go borrow something of mine."

With a silent growl, Mandy took the stairs two at a time and shuffled through her mother's jewelry box, deciding quickly to borrow her pearl earrings. Once she was back downstairs, her mother insisted she light a fire in the fireplace so Mandy trudged outside and dragged in a few sticks of firewood and got a fire going.

Five minutes after six o'clock, Mandy's heart jolted at the sound of the knock at the door. She rushed downstairs and took a breath before opening the door.

There stood Leo. Mandy was glad he couldn't see her heart skip a beat.

Come on, Mandy, calm down. Don't get so excited.

"One chef at your service, ma'am," Leo said. Mandy beamed back at him.

"Come in, Mr. Romano. I'm very glad to see you."

Mandy opened the door and motioned for Leo to come in. He held two stuffed grocery bags in his arms and she took one from him.

"Are you sure you're up for this?" Mandy whispered, leading him down the hallway. Leo looked at her, puzzled.

"What do you mean?"

"Meeting my mother. Are you sure you're ready for this?"

The confident, self-assured look in Leo's eyes was enough to make Mandy's heart pound.

"I'm ready, Mandy."

Leo's tone seemed so unquestionable that Mandy had to wonder just what he was ready for. To meet her mother? Or something more?

After setting the bags down on the kitchen island, Mandy led Leo to where her mother was sitting on the sofa.

"Leo, this is my mother, Claire Seymour. Mom, this is Leonardo Romano."

Leo held out his hand and shook her mother's warmly. His dark eyes focused solely on Claire.

"Mrs. Seymour, it's a pleasure to meet you. Please call me Leo."

With one look, Mandy knew her mother was more than impressed.

Of course, he's gorgeous and well mannered. Who wouldn't be impressed? Wait till she tastes his cooking.

"Welcome, Leo. And please call me Claire. Make yourself at home here. My kitchen is yours tonight."

Mandy's heart softened at her mother's hospitality and the kindness in her voice.

My mother, the consummate hostess.

"Thank you," Leo said before turning his gaze to Mandy. "Come along, Mandy."

Mandy blinked. "What?"

"I need a sous chef so…I need you."

That was a loaded statement. He's either flirting with me or he's unaware of how appealing he is.

Mandy licked her lips and smiled back, hoping he didn't have an idea of how strongly he affected her.

"Well, then, chef, I'm yours," she said, her voice light and carefree.

Two can play at this game, Mr. Romano.

* * *

Mandy inhaled the smell of garlic and listened to the sound of breaded chicken cutlets frying in olive oil.

"Keep chopping," Leo ordered as he kneaded the dough in front of him.

Mandy suppressed a chuckle at Leo's bossiness. There was no mistaking his chef status in the kitchen. She finished chopping one tomato and reached for an onion. Leo watched as she minced the onion.

"Where did you learn to do that?" Leo asked, obviously impressed. Mandy shrugged.

"My mother."

"You're an even better sous chef than I expected."

"I love to cook. I just wish I had more time to practice." Mandy held back from telling him what she was really thinking: that working side by side with him in the kitchen felt wonderful. She loved the easy way they worked together, the comfortable moments of silence, the look on Leo's face as he concentrated on the task in front of him, how strong and yet graceful his hands were as they prepared dinner.

"Mandy, drain the pasta…please," Leo said, his eyes focused on the dough. His almost-black hair fell over his forehead in a way that made Mandy want to reach over and brush it back.

"I hope you don't mind that I brought dessert already made," Leo said as Mandy strained the boiling water from the spaghetti noodles.

"Since you brought tiramisu, which, as you know, is one of my weaknesses, I can forgive you this time." From where she stood at the sink, Mandy looked over her shoulder at him. He stopped what he was doing and looked straight back at her.

In that moment, inundated by mouth-watering smells of fresh mozzarella, parmesan and onion, the look in Leo's dark eyes made Mandy's mouth go dry. He left what he

was doing and moved next to her, pausing to stir the tomato
sauce simmering on the stove.

"Taste this for me, Mandy," he said, holding the spoon
out to her.

*Those just might be the most romantic words that have
ever been spoken to me.*

Mandy tasted the sauce and licked her lips. "Perfect."

Leo grinned. "Good."

"Aren't you going to taste it?" Mandy wondered. Leo
shook his head.

"I don't need to. If Mandy Seymour, respected food
critic, tells me it's delicious—then I know it's ready."

Mandy blushed and looked back down at the bubbling
tomato sauce. "So you trust me when it comes to tomato
sauce?" she quipped.

Leo tucked a strand of Mandy's hair behind her ear.

"Among other things. Do you trust me, Mandy?" Leo
asked in a low voice. Mandy stared up at him, enjoying the
close proximity to him and the playful look in his eyes.

"Only when it comes to tomato sauce," she said with an
impish smile.

Leo looked down at his cell phone in frustration. This
was the third call he'd received in two hours. He leaned
against the counter and answered the phone, watching
Mandy carry dishes of chicken parmesan to the dining
room table.

"Angelina, what's up?" Leo asked, being careful to keep
the annoyance out of his voice.

"Leo, we've got a guy here whose credit card has been
declined. Actually, every card he's given us has been declined."

"Is it a large order?"

"Just over a hundred dollars."

Leo groaned. "Okay. Ask for a business card, his driver's

license and a phone number. Take down all his information. Tell him to come back and pay with cash by tomorrow or we will have to involve the police."

"Got it. Hey, sorry to keep interrupting the date. How's it going?"

"Bye, Angie."

Leo could hear his cousin giggle as he hung up the phone. He tucked his phone back into his pocket and joined Mandy and her mother at the table.

"May I pray for us?" Leo asked. He saw the surprise on Claire's face as she smiled and nodded. After blessing the food, Leo passed the main-course platter to Claire first. He watched intently as she took her first bite. There was always something about that first bite—Leo could see whether he'd created a masterpiece or just a mediocre dish. The way Claire's eyes closed and her sigh told Leo everything he needed to know. He grinned in satisfaction.

"Delicious!" Claire exclaimed. Mandy took a small bite and complimented Leo, as well, but something felt off. Leo knew without a doubt that Mandy's sensitive palate would appreciate the flavors of the meal so he wasn't sure what the problem was.

It didn't take long for him to figure it out.

Claire's presence restricted Mandy. Her conversation, the small portions that Mandy ate—everything seemed constrained compared to their evening together at El Camino Blanco. The way Mandy glanced at her mother frequently, followed her mother's lead in conversation and hesitated before reaching for a platter.

"I never thanked you, Mandy," Leo said suddenly. Mandy seemed confused.

"For what, Leo?"

"For helping out at Romano's the other night."

Mandy blushed. "Liz told you."

Leo tore a piece of garlic bread in half and handed one

half to Mandy. She hesitated for a moment before taking it from him, their fingers brushing each other. Leo liked the feeling of sharing with her. It reminded him of that first night when they'd shared dessert.

"We were having a really rough night at both restaurants, we were short-staffed and one of our main chefs went home ill. Everything that could go wrong, went wrong. Mandy was at our Franklin location. After closing, she stayed and helped clean up," Leo explained to Claire. He looked over at Mandy and found it hard to look away. Her hair fell softly over her shoulders. The freckles scattered over her nose combined with her expressive eyes fascinated him. "You didn't have to. Why did you stay?"

Mandy shrugged. "You needed help."

Leo felt a lump in his throat and quickly reached for his glass of water.

Those few words were so much more accurate than she could know. With everything going on in his life, Leo felt as though he were desperate for help.

"Your daughter is a very special woman," Leo said, hoping neither Claire nor Mandy noticed the catch in his voice.

Claire was quiet for a moment.

"Yes, she is."

After that, Leo felt a shift in the atmosphere. Mandy seemed to relax somewhat. By the time Mandy served the tiramisu, the mood at the table was one of enjoyment.

Leo thought of his dad. Gabriel Romano believed that dining should be enjoyed, that food should bring people together. In that moment, it occurred to Leo how important those things were to him, too. As clear as day, Leo could remember time and again, his mother cupping his face in her hands and saying, "You are your father's son, Leonardo."

He used to feel aggravated when his mother would say that. The phrase made him bristle, as though he were just a copy of his dad; it left no room for his individuality. But as the years passed, Leo had found it to be the highest compliment he could receive. And more true than not.

As he sat watching Mandy interact with her mother, Leo could instinctively gather that Claire's opinion mattered more to Mandy than she would ever admit. Didn't her mother realize how unique Mandy was? How talented, gifted and special Mandy was?

From the outside looking in, Leo had no doubt it would take much more time—and openness on Mandy's part—for him to understand the layers of Mandy's relationship with her mother. But he knew one thing: He wanted Mandy to know that *he* saw those things in her.

They'd moved to the living room to enjoy their coffee. Leo accepted the cup that Mandy offered him. In some ways, Mandy reminded him of his own mother—an excellent hostess with a servant's heart.

As his cell phone rang once more, Leo felt torn between his guilt for not being at the restaurants when he was needed and his increasing desire to stay in Mandy Seymour's presence as long as possible.

Chapter 9

By the time Leo left, Mandy knew he'd won her mother over completely. The three of them had sat in front of the fireplace, drinking decaf French vanilla coffee and chatting for nearly forty-five minutes. Mandy and Claire had listened as Leo talked about his parents and his sister, life as a restaurant owner, his favorite dishes and the things he loved most about living in Colorado.

At one point, Mandy feared that her mother was asking Leo too many questions about himself, but his engaged and affable manner set her mind at ease. Mandy appreciated his sociable and outgoing style. Rather than being shy or withdrawn, Leo easily made conversation and could definitely captivate an audience with his warm charm.

In short, he had all the qualities of the type of man Mandy found herself attracted to.

As they'd stood on the front porch to say goodbye, the air so cold that Mandy could see her breath, she'd felt a surge of hopefulness that Leo might kiss her. If she was reading him correctly, the look in his eyes conveyed to her that he wanted to kiss her just as badly. But he'd simply hugged her and promised to call her soon.

Mandy locked the door behind Leo and walked back through the quiet house. Her mother had gone up to bed, giving Mandy a perfect opportunity to analyze every moment of the evening. Mandy rather wished that Ashley was with her to talk through each detail. She poured herself another cup of coffee, curled up on the sofa and opened her heart to pray.

Father, I'm just a little concerned that Leo is too perfect. I'm not really sure what he sees in me. When I look at him, I see a man who's handsome and talented and family oriented—and someone who could have any woman he wants. So why is he spending time with me? I keep telling myself not to fall too hard because I just might get my heart broken.

Mandy didn't hear any voices from heaven dispelling her uncertainty, but a sense of peace that she knew came from God washed over her and filled her with contentment.

The next morning, Mandy came downstairs to find her mother already in the kitchen, stirring a pot of oatmeal.

"You must be feeling better!" Mandy exclaimed.

Claire motioned for Mandy to sit down at the breakfast table. "I am. My back is still tender, but I'm feeling better today. I know you need to get back to Denver. You have your work. And besides, your father will be home this afternoon."

Mandy accepted the bowl her mother handed her. She couldn't help feeling nostalgic for all the mornings she'd spent as a little girl, eating oatmeal for breakfast. She still loved her mother's blend of cinnamon and sugar and raisins mixed into the thick porridge.

"What did you think of Leo?" Mandy wondered. Her mother poured two glasses of orange juice and then gingerly sat down in the seat across from Mandy.

"Well, he's wonderful," she said. Her mother's eyes twinkled.

"Oh, good. I was worried you wouldn't like him," Mandy laughed. But her laughter faded as she again wondered what Leo liked about her and whether he had any serious intentions toward her. "You're probably wondering what he sees in me," Mandy said.

Claire frowned. "I know what he sees in you, Amanda," her mother said. "And it's what I've, unfortunately, overlooked at times when I should have been the first one to tell you. He sees what I see—a beautiful, capable woman with a sweet, compassionate spirit and a heart to please God. That's who you are, Mandy."

Mandy didn't want to cry, but she found herself unable to hold back her tears. She'd waited years to hear her mother say those things, and the fact that they were obviously being spoken with sincerity made the walls surrounding Mandy's heart crumble. She looked straight at her mother, her heart so full it hurt.

"To be honest, Mom, what Leo sees when he looks at me isn't as important to me as what you see."

Her mother reached across the table and touched Mandy's hand.

"You're one more thing, Amanda."

"What's that?"

"You're my daughter, and I'm proud of you. It's clear I haven't said that enough. But it's true."

Leo leaned closer to his laptop, looking over the latest financial report for the Franklin Romano's. Unsurprisingly, the restaurant was doing well. Year after year, his father's restaurant flourished. What *did* surprise Leo was how well his own Romano's location was doing. The restaurant was off to a tremendous start, no doubt partly because of the connection to the Franklin restaurant. But in the current economic climate, with so many businesses struggling, the success of his restaurant astounded him. And worried him. With both restaurants doing so well, he couldn't realistically entertain the thought of closing one of them.

Leo pushed his chair back and swiveled around in his

father's office, looking over the decor his mother had chosen. A knock at the door caught his attention. Leo stood up as Isabella walked in.

"Hey, bro."

Leo grinned and sat back down. "What brings you here?"

Isa plopped down in the chair across from him. "Free lunch. I have to work at two o'clock so I thought I'd stop by and see if my big brother would feed me."

Twenty minutes later, the two of them were seated at a booth in the back of the restaurant, eating salami and cheese panini sandwiches and drinking sodas. Leo couldn't begin to count the number of times he and Isa had had this same experience.

"You haven't made any changes to the office," Isa mentioned and Leo shrugged.

"I hate to make changes to things Mom decorated."

Isa shrugged. "So ask Mom to redecorate for you. She would love to feel included. Give her some direction and let her go for it. You know she'll do a great job."

Leo rubbed his chin. "Why didn't I think of that? Good idea, sis."

Isa nodded. "What else do you need my help with?"

Leo took a swig of his Coke and folded his arms across his chest. "Tell me how to find time for a social life in between running two restaurants."

Isa looked at him with sympathy. "I know it's not easy. Delegate, Leo. Ask for help. Bring in good people. Hire another manager. Dad constantly struggled with balancing family life and work. Sometimes he succeeded, sometimes he didn't. No one expects you to be perfect at this."

"I don't want to fail him."

Leo watched Isa pause as those words sank in. She reached across the table and rested her hand on his arm.

"I promise that you won't, Leo."

"There's one more thing you can help me with, Isa," Leo stated.

"Bring it on. What can I do?"

"I'm planning to bring a new friend to family dinner Monday night. Be nice to her. I want her to feel welcome."

Isa's mouth fell open. "You're dating someone? And no one told me?"

Leo chuckled. "Yes and yes."

Isa's eyes softened and Leo could see relief on her face. He knew she'd been praying for months for him to move on from his broken engagement. The realization of that stopped him in his tracks: In a very real sense, Mandy was an answer to a prayer.

"So who is she?" Isa pressed.

"Mandy Seymour, a food critic for *Denver Lifestyle* magazine. I'm taking things slowly—"

"Perfect," Isa groaned. "Every girl wants a guy who moves at the pace of a turtle."

Leo burst out laughing. "Not *that* slowly. Hey, I'm inviting her to family dinner! That's something."

Isa nodded, her eyes dancing. "True. And I can't wait to meet her."

After Isa left, Leo called his mother and asked her to redecorate the office. The sheer happiness in his mother's voice told him that he owed Isa big-time for that idea. With that conversation out of the way, he dialed Mandy's phone number.

"Mandy Seymour," she answered.

"Did I catch you at the office?" Leo asked.

"Leo, hi. Yes, you did. But that's okay. I mean, you can call me anytime," she stammered.

Leo stood up and paced the length of the office, trying to quell the delight that he felt from just hearing Mandy say his name.

"Are you interested in having dinner with my family and me Monday night?"

"Yes."

Her answer was so automatic that Leo guessed Mandy felt the same delight that he did.

"You're sure?" Leo said.

"Of course. Can I ask your dad for his autograph?"

Leo laughed. "Should I be jealous?"

"Probably."

"We'll have to work on that. I'll text you the directions. Dinner usually begins around seven-thirty."

"Sounds wonderful. Thank you for inviting me. Can I bring anything?"

The kindness in Mandy's voice swept over Leo like a warm blanket.

"No. Just you."

Leo was still smiling long after the phone call had ended. He finished going over financial statements, his employee payroll, his personal investments, the menus for both restaurants and the inventory list for the kitchen. He spent over an hour carefully reviewing résumés that had come in from potential chefs for the Fifteenth Street restaurant.

By the time the evening rush began, he wished he'd reserved some energy for cooking. He drove to the Fifteenth Street restaurant and walked into the kitchen, already tired and knowing he had hours to go before he could rest.

Sunday after church, Ashley invaded Mandy's closet. Mandy sat cross-legged on her bed while Ashley stood scowling.

"When was the last time you went shopping, Mandy Seymour? 'Cause I'm thinking it was around 1998."

Mandy ignored Ashley's melodrama since the two of them had gone shopping together just a few weeks before.

"It's Colorado, Ash. It's cold. There's snow out there.

My options are jeans…or jeans. I'm thinking jeans. Your thoughts?"

Ashley sighed. "No jeans. You can wear your black dress with stockings and dangly earrings."

"It's family dinner. What if everyone else is super casual?"

"So ask Leo."

"We're not there yet."

"You're not where? To the place where you can ask him if 'family dinner' is casual?"

Mandy fell back on her pillows. "Fine. I'll text him and see what he says." Mandy grabbed her phone and punched in a message to Leo.

Family dinner…casual?

Within a minute, her phone beeped with an incoming text.

Yes.

Mandy thought for a moment.
She texted back. How casual?
Again, the response was nearly instantaneous.

You can wear whatever you want.

Mandy showed Ashley the text and Ashley rolled her eyes. "Very helpful. You're meeting the family. How casual do you want to be?"

"Well, I don't want to look like I'm ready for an Easter Sunday service while everyone else is in T-shirts."

Ashley tilted her head to the side. "Fine. I'll think of something." She turned back to sift through Mandy's clothes.

"Ash?"

"Hmm?"

"Do you think this is all happening too fast? I mean, we just had our first date not that long ago. Then he meets my mom. Now I'm meeting his family. I'm just a little nervous about all this. I told you about his broken engagement. Maybe he's just lonely and this is a rebound thing."

The bed creaked as Ashley sat down next to her.

"Honey, don't do this."

Mandy looked up. "Do what?"

"You know. Don't sell yourself short, don't let your insecurities get in the way of something that might be fabulous."

"I just feel… I'm not sure why he likes me. Or if he's serious about this."

Ashley shook her hair back. "All right. Listen up. Time for one of my famous pep talks."

Mandy closed her eyes and motioned for Ashley to continue.

"One, I don't think he'd bother introducing you to the family if the boy didn't have some serious intentions. C'mon, he drove to Evergreen to cook you dinner. That spells love in any language. Two, he likes you because you're likable. I mean, sweetie, you are a great catch."

Mandy snorted at that comment.

"Three, if it lasts or if it doesn't—you have to take this risk for one important reason."

Mandy frowned and opened one eye. "What's that?"

"Because you're borderline nuts about him. And you'd be crazy not to be. Don't be such a scaredy-cat, Miss Seymour. And if it doesn't work out, tell Mr. Tall, Dark and Handsome to call me."

Mandy double-checked her GPS to make sure she was in the right place. She and Ashley had compromised and

Mandy felt as comfortable as she could hope to be in her favorite gray pants, a black sweater and dangly earrings.

The Romano home perched on a hill, with a perfect view of the mountains. A line of cars crowded the circular driveway. Mandy took a deep breath before leaving her car and walking toward the large home. She knocked once and the door swung open. A dark-haired young woman who resembled Leo stood in front of her with a wide smile on her face.

"Mandy Seymour, welcome. I'm Isabella Romano, Leo's sister. Please call me Isa. Leo's told me all about you. I'm under strict instructions to stay by your side. So come on in!" She stepped aside and Mandy walked through the door. The sounds of voices and music drifted through the house.

"Is Leo here?" Mandy asked, trying to keep the nervousness from her voice.

"He's running late."

What!

"Don't worry. He'll be here any minute. Come meet everybody."

Meet everybody?

Mandy gritted her teeth, promising herself that she could be mad at Leo later. Right now, she was about to meet his family and needed to appear perfectly calm and relaxed. Isa led her down a hallway into the kitchen. Mandy froze, feeling as if she'd entered a scene from a movie. People filled the kitchen from one corner to the other, laughing, talking—Mandy noticed that several conversations were in Italian. But, as if a switch had been flipped, the room fell silent and every eye was on her.

"This is Mandy, Leo's friend," Isa explained. Surprise dawned on most faces, but one petite woman who could only have been Leo's mother stepped forward.

"I'm Rosalinda. Mandy, tonight, you are family. Welcome." She pulled Mandy into a gentle hug.

The swoop of silence was replaced with the chatter of at

least fifteen voices speaking at once. Mandy tried to keep up as people introduced themselves. Isa stayed at her side, giving Mandy the support she needed.

"Hey."

Mandy turned around, relieved to see Leo, but she hoped the "You're in trouble" look she was giving him was registering.

He grinned and leaned down by her ear. "Yes, you can yell at me later. I'm sorry I'm late. Last-minute stuff at the restaurant. Now, there's someone I want you to meet."

Mandy nodded. Delicious tingles shot up her arm as Leo took her hand and laced their fingers together. He guided her through the crowd to the kitchen table where the one and only Gabriel Romano sat.

"Dad, this is Mandy."

Gabriel Romano looked like an older version of Leo, handsome with vibrant eyes, silver hair and a charming smile. He reached a wavering hand out to Mandy, and pain shot through her heart.

Why? I just met him.

Mandy held his hand and looked right into his eyes and she understood her reaction.

It's because of Leo, isn't it, Father? I already feel so connected to him that seeing his dad this way hurts me, too.

The thought unnerved Mandy. Without waiting for Leo, she pulled out a chair and sat down next to Gabriel.

"I fell in love with your tiramisu a long time ago, Mr. Romano."

The beaming look on Gabriel's face told Mandy she'd made an instant friend.

"Call me Gabriel. Let's hope you fall in love with my son."

Mandy's face turned bright red, but probably not as scarlet as Leo's.

"Dad!"

Gabriel waved him off without a glance. "I'm talking with Mandy. Go help your sister with the lasagna."

Leo raised his eyebrows at Mandy and she knew he wouldn't leave her unless she gave him the okay to do so. She nodded and smiled and he headed toward the stove, calling out for Angelina to set the table. Mandy recognized Angelina as the server from Leo's restaurant. It seemed that every inch of the Romano home buzzed with activity. The room radiated warmth, no doubt a result of the hot stoves and large crowd.

"Now, Mandy, tell me, do you love Jesus?"

Mandy blinked in surprise. "I do," she answered.

"Good, good. Do you love food?" he asked and Mandy burst into giggles.

"Absolutely."

"Those are the only two requisites for joining our family."

"Well, I'm in, then," Mandy responded and Gabriel laughed loudly. As their laughter died down, Gabriel patted her hand and lowered his voice.

"I'm sure Leo has told you of his disappointment—his broken engagement."

Mandy nodded, glancing back toward where Leo stood slicing a loaf of bread and simultaneously arguing with an older woman in Italian. He caught her eye and winked.

He speaks Italian? How did I not know that?

"I'm sure that was difficult for him," Mandy said, her gaze still on Leo.

Gabriel's eyes saddened. "Yes, it was. As it would be for anyone. But Leo is strong, stronger than he knows. And God has a plan for his life. I was so glad to hear that Leonardo was bringing a guest tonight. It's been a long time. In fact, he's only ever brought one other girl to family dinner...and he thought he would marry her. I believe you must be very special, Mandy."

Those words seemed to hover over Mandy before plunging into her. Along with the understanding that bringing her to meet Leo's family meant more than she realized, Gabriel's comment that she must be very special touched that vulnerable place inside in Mandy that always resisted believing that sort of thing.

Mandy looked around at the bustling room, thinking about how much she was enjoying this moment, surrounded by the energy and vitality of the Romano family, taking in the essence of everything that made Leo…Leo.

Mandy turned her attention back to Gabriel. "Romano's is such a phenomenal restaurant, Mr. Rom—Gabriel. It's one of my favorites, and believe me when I say I've tried nearly all the restaurants in Denver. You have a true gift for creating great food."

Gabriel's hands jerked and Mandy noticed the tremors go up his arms.

"God allowed me to use my hands for many years to pursue my passion to cook, to create food that would bring people together. But ever since he was a child, we all knew that this was Leo's gift, as well. He was creating culinary masterpieces before he knew that that's what they were. This is his time now. I only hope it's not too much for him. I know from experience how demanding restaurant life can be."

"He can do it."

Mandy looked to her right as Leo's mother joined the conversation. Rosalinda placed her hands on her husband's shoulders. "Leo's enthusiasm for cooking matches his father's. Not to mention his talent," she told Mandy. "Sometimes administration and leadership have to go along with the role of a good chef. But other than Gabriel, my son is the most capable man I know. He'll rise to the occasion."

Rosalinda leaned down to speak in Gabriel's ear. "Gabriel, it's time for your medication. Should I bring it to you?"

He shook his head. Leo walked back over to the table, drying his hands on a dish towel.

"Leo, help me up to my room, son. I'm feeling tired all of a sudden and I think I'd like to lie down after I take my medication."

Mandy watched as Leo's brow furrowed with concern. He tossed the dish towel on the counter and helped his dad stand up.

"I'll be back, Mandy," Leo said. Within seconds Isa was right at Leo's side.

"Dad?" she said, taking his other arm. "Are you all right?"

"I'm fine. I'm sorry, Mandy," Gabriel said with a tired smile. "My family likes to make a fuss over me."

"Of course they do," Mandy said. Leo and Isa walked on either side of Gabriel through the kitchen.

"When his hands start to shake, it becomes somewhat difficult for Gabriel to feed himself," Leo's mother murmured, her eyes following Gabriel. "He still manages when we're home by ourselves. But sometimes it makes him uncomfortable in a gathering like this."

Mandy's heart ached for Gabriel, for Leo, for all of them.

"He's a remarkable man," Mandy said softly, thinking of Gabriel's talents, his success, but more than anything, his beautiful, loving family.

Rosalinda looked at Mandy with a tender smile. "Yes. And Leonardo is just like him."

Mandy watched as Leo walked down the hallway with his dad, and the feeling that came over her as she stared at Leo felt suspiciously like love. "Yes, I can see that."

Chapter 10

Mandy was halfway through the most scrumptious plate of lasagna she'd ever tasted, trying to follow two conversations. Across the table, Leo's twenty-year-old cousin, Nick, hadn't stopped talking about his new car. On Mandy's left, Isa was talking about the frustrations of working the night shift at the hospital.

By the second time Leo excused himself to return a call to the restaurant, Mandy knew something was wrong. He slid back on the wooden bench seat next to her.

"Leo, what's up?" Mandy whispered.

"It's Monday night—usually our slowest night. Caitlyn, our seating hostess at the Franklin location tonight, called because we've had two large-party walk-ins. When I say large, I mean one of the parties has nearly forty people. So the cooks are scrambling…there aren't enough people. They need help."

"Then let's go," Mandy said immediately.

"I hate to do that to you," Leo said, his forehead creased with anxiety. Mandy shrugged.

"I'm the one suggesting it. You need to be there. We should go."

Leo sighed but Mandy knew he agreed. After a round of goodbyes, Leo walked Mandy out to her car.

"So I'll call you," he told her.

"I'll meet you at the restaurant," she insisted. Leo shook his head.

"Mandy, you don't need to go to the restaurant with me."

Mandy didn't want to add to Leo's angst, but she couldn't stand the thought of just going home while he walked head-on into a stressful situation.

"I want to help, Leo. I'll wash dishes, wait tables, refill water glasses, whatever you want me to do."

He crossed his arms and looked at her quizzically. "Do you have any experience, Ms. Seymour?"

Mandy chuckled. "Do two years as a waitress during college count?"

The corners of Leo's mouth tilted up. "You're hired."

By nine o'clock that night, the orders began to let up, allowing Leo, Adam and Crey to breathe easier. Leo had been informed that Mandy had bused tables, refilled drinks and bread trays, and cleaned the ladies' room sink.

He could have loved her just for that.

Leo didn't want to make comparisons, but it had crossed his mind more than once that Carol Ann had never offered to help out at the restaurant. Granted, he wasn't the owner at the time. But he'd always been heavily involved and there were so many hectic nights working with his father.

Thinking of Mandy going from table to table—even busing tables when the others were busy—made Leo want to drop everything, take her in his arms and tell her that she was exactly what he needed in his life.

But he couldn't.

I couldn't even make it through a Monday-night family dinner. How do I make room in my life for a relationship? Especially when I know that, for me, a relationship with Mandy could only be enough if I marry her. She's not the kind of girl I just want to date. I know I would need more, want more.

Once the doors were locked, Leo watched as Mandy laughed and joked with the staff. He recalled the way she pulled up a chair and sat down right next to his father at the family dinner, talking as if they were old friends.

His chest tightened. After the disaster with Carol Ann, he'd sworn that he'd take his next relationship as slow as possible. So why did being around Mandy make him want to rush into things? He wanted fast and furious, not slow and steady.

Annoyance rose in Leo. Why would God bring Mandy into his life right now when he felt pulled in every direction? It seemed that either God was throwing everything He could think of at Leo, or He wasn't involved at all.

Leo didn't know which was worse: the thought that God was doing this to him, or that God didn't care.

As he walked Mandy to her car at nearly eleven o'clock, Leo sternly reminded himself of his list of obligations at the moment and his need to keep his head about him whenever he was alone with Mandy. The last thing he wanted was to lead her into thinking he could foster a serious relationship with her.

Haven't I already done that? Asking her to dinner? Introducing her to my family?

The thought disheartened him.

Starting right now I'm going to keep my distance. I'll be her friend, but I can't offer more than that until things calm down with the restaurants and my family.

Mandy unlocked her car and tossed her purse into the passenger seat, then turned and faced Leo. Even exhaustion couldn't take the shine out of her eyes.

"Leo—" she began. His stern admonishment to himself vanished and Leo didn't hesitate. He stopped her words with a kiss. It took only a second for Mandy's restraint to melt away as she seemed to fold into his arms.

When he finally found the willpower to release her, Leo felt more overwhelmed than before.

He'd just fallen hard and fast for Mandy Seymour. So much for restraint.

Mandy drove home, her heart racing.

It was just a kiss, after all, she told herself again and again. *It's not as though the world has stopped.*

But it had, and Mandy knew it. Her world stopped when Leonardo Romano invaded her personal space and kissed her, leaving her breathless. She touched her lips. A smile that started deep inside her made its way to the surface as she recalled that he smelled like marinara sauce.

The text at 7:00 a.m. came as a surprise. Mandy could sense the urgency in the short message from Leo, asking her to meet him for coffee. She got ready in a flash and left for Starbucks by seven forty-five. When she walked in, he was standing by the door.

The circles under his eyes caused Mandy to wonder whether he'd slept at all.

"Leo?" She approached him. Unfortunately, Starbucks in the morning was a constant revolving door of people. "Let's step outside," Mandy offered. Leo's glossy eyes worried her.

"It's cold," he said, his voice thick with fatigue. Mandy took his hand.

"We can talk in my car, then. Come on."

Once they were in her car, the heater warming them both, Mandy spoke up.

"You might as well tell me, Leo. Something is obviously wrong."

He looked rugged and tired and unshaven, but Mandy couldn't help feeling attracted to him. Still, she wasn't the kind of girl to let her feelings run away with her. She swallowed her impulse to reach over and lace their fingers together.

"Talk to me, Leo."

He groaned. "I feel like I can't breathe, Mandy. The restaurants. My dad. God. My family. You."

The words stung. He'd added her to the list like another obligation.

"I know you're going through a lot right now," she said as calmly as she could manage. "I told you that before. Are you saying you don't want to pursue a relationship right now?" Mandy forced herself to ask the question.

"I want that more than anything," Leo said, almost angrily. "I just don't see how it can work. It seems like God's decided to give me more than I can take right now."

Mandy was quiet for a moment. "God doesn't give us more than we can take, Leo."

He narrowed his eyes. "Tell me that when your dad has Parkinson's, when you're trying to juggle two restaurants, when you're constantly getting phone calls to either drop everything and run to the hospital, or drop everything and run to your restaurant. When your family is counting on you but you have nothing left."

Mandy felt the fight leave her.

"Leo, all those things you just said—you didn't mention God once. He's not doing those things to you. You could sell the restaurants tomorrow and decide to do something totally different with your life, and He'd still be right there, walking with you on your journey. I definitely don't believe He brought on your father's illness. He loves your Dad even more than you do."

"Maybe He's not causing it—but He's letting it all happen. He's just standing by while my father struggles with a debilitating disease that will continue to cripple him." Pain saturated Leo's words.

Mandy reached over and squeezed his arm. "I'm so sorry.

The truth is that I can only imagine the hurt you feel about your dad right now. But I *do* know what it's like to wonder where God is in your life, to wonder why He doesn't seem to show up when you need rescuing."

Leo lost his pained expression and looked at her with interest. "It sounds like you have personal experience. Want to tell me about it, Mandy?"

Mandy looked out the car window as snow began to drift down. Years of self-doubt, dismissal and heartache influenced her next words. "It wasn't one thing that happened. It was moments piled on top of moments, starting way back in junior high—maybe even earlier than that. There were times when I was bullied in school, made fun of, laughed at. I learned to mask the hurt with humor, but that was only a mask. I was a senior in college before anyone ever asked me on a date. For a really long time I felt rejected and worthless. Even at home, I…well, I never felt good enough. Never accepted for who I was. So believe me when I tell you I've wondered why God lets bad things happen."

"How did you get past it?"

Mandy exhaled. "It's amazing, you know. We can rant at God, and in the same breath, beg Him for comfort. We can feel angry with God, and at the same time, desperate for Him. Even in those times when I felt as though God was nowhere near me, I'd find myself turning to Him, calling out to Him. Sometimes that's all we can do. As far as I can tell, it's not about 'getting past it—' it's just a matter of trusting through it. Reaching out when it hurts. At least, that's been my experience. In moments when I've felt alone, like I'm a total failure, and disappointed with my circumstances, I know I can pour out all those emotions before God. He's big enough to handle it."

"Sometimes I feel so guilty for doubting, for being angry," Leo confessed.

"I know that feeling, too. It's okay, Leo," Mandy said. After a moment of silence, Leo started talking.

"I care about you, Mandy. But right now, I just don't think I can manage a relationship. I'm sorry."

It sounded as though his words carried the heaviness of regret, but he'd said them nonetheless. Only the gentle whirring of the heater broke the silence. Mandy reminded herself to breathe. She'd had a feeling something along those lines was coming, but she hadn't expected to feel so hollow when Leo said the words. She hadn't realized she was already so invested. She heard herself tell Leo that she understood and then heard him say something about how much he cared about her and that this wasn't goodbye forever.

Mandy concentrated on holding it together until he'd left the car. She drove to work, willing herself not to cry. But along with Leo's insistence that he couldn't pursue a relationship with her now, came a flood of old feelings that Mandy could hardly stand—disappointment, hurt and most of all, rejection.

Chapter 11

Mandy yelped and drew her hand away from the boiling pot.

"Mandy? What happened?" Ashley dashed into the kitchen. Mandy sucked on the tip of her throbbing finger and shook her head.

"Me! I'm such a klutz. I just burned my finger." At that moment, boiling water bubbled over the pot and water began sizzling on the stove. Mandy jumped and as she reached for the handle to lift the pot away from the burner, her elbow knocked the cookbook from the counter to the floor, along with a saltshaker. White grains of salt shot out across the tiled floor.

At that, Mandy broke down. She covered her face with her hands and cried. Silently, Ashley turned down the burner and moved the pot of boiling water. She picked up the recipe book and draped one arm around Mandy's shoulders.

"There, there, sweetie. Let's go sit down. Forget dinner. I'll order takeout from that Thai place you like. Though heaven knows what I'll order. I hope everything's not drenched in curry."

Mandy allowed Ashley to direct her to the sofa and wrap a fleece blanket around her. She tried to stop crying as

Ashley disappeared into the kitchen to call for takeout, but stubborn tears were still escaping when Ashley rejoined her on the sofa.

"Honey, you can cry all you want."

"I don't want to cry at all."

"Well, you've got the Niagara Falls look goin' at the moment that begs to differ," Ashley replied.

"This is silly. It's not like we were in a serious relationship. I've only known him for a few weeks, really. We had a few dates, he cooked for me, he invited me to dinner with his family and he kissed me once."

"It's not silly. You care about him. He's putting the brakes on this thing and you have every right to be disappointed about that. Good grief, *I'm* disappointed."

Mandy sighed loudly and rested her head on the sofa. "I don't know why I'm surprised. First of all, I have the worst luck of anyone I know. Second, he's out of my league."

Ashley shook her head furiously. "Say that again and I'll pinch you. Have a little faith, girlfriend. Okay, your luck might be questionable—it's hard to argue that point—but it's ridiculous to think he's out of your league because he's not and you know it. He's got a lot on his plate right now, Mandy. Let's wait and see what happens. I don't know about you, but I don't think we've heard the last from Leonardo Romano."

Mandy reached for the tissue box on the end table and one thought went through her mind.

Oh, I sincerely hope not.

Leo sat at the wooden table in his parents' home, sipping a cappuccino and poring over his father's Italian recipe books. Most were older than Leo was. His father had brought them home from Italy when he was a young man, just starting out in the restaurant business.

"What's happening with that lovely young woman we met, Leo?"

He shrugged as his mother walked through the kitchen and joined him at the table.

"Not much. You know I don't have time for that kind of thing right now, Mom."

His mom looked amused. "What kind of thing are we talking about?"

"A relationship. Romance. Commitment. I don't have room for those things right now. I wish I did, okay? But I don't," Leo said tersely.

"Ah," his mother said, unperturbed. "Yes, I see. And believe me, I understand. Your father has owned two restaurants for more than a decade, and it hasn't been easy. Now you own two restaurants. The responsibility is enormous. The pressure is great." His mother folded her hands on the table and looked Leo straight in the eyes. "But, Leo, if you let them become your whole life, you'll hate the restaurants, rather than appreciate them. There were times when your father had more of a love-hate relationship with his businesses. And I had those times, too. But in the end, he loved Romano's. He still does. It's part of him. It's the source that supported his family."

Leo pushed aside his cappuccino and rested his head in his hands. "Mom," he moaned, "it's more stress than I ever expected. I've always known I'd take over Romano's when the time came. I didn't expect to have this second restaurant, but that's all right. But trying to keep everything afloat while Dad… While he—" Leo lost his words. His mother took both of Leo's hands in hers.

"Your father is here with us. I thank God *every day* for that, for every moment I have him in my life. And I feel honored and blessed to serve my husband, to help him through this. We are not the only family with illness, Leo. But how many families do you know that have the kind of love we have for each other? It's a gift. Our family is a gift from God."

Leo tried to swallow but the well of emotion in his throat choked him.

"Why isn't God helping us? Why isn't God healing Dad?"

His mother straightened her shoulders and spoke with conviction. "I don't know why he hasn't healed Gabriel. But I can say with certainty that he's been helping us. When my heart has been broken, I've felt God's comfort. When I'm unsure about your father's treatments or confused by his disease, my daughter has been there to patiently explain, to help me understand. God's helped me through Isabella. And God gave me a son who was able to step in and take over when his father couldn't work anymore. God helps me every day through you, Leo."

Leo sat motionless, humbled by his mother's admission.

"God might be trying to help you now, Leo, by bringing someone into your life who can offer support and even love."

Leo shook his head. "I care about Mandy too much to burden her with all the stress of my life right now."

Leo recognized the exasperation in his mother's countenance. "It's your decision, of course, Leonardo. But right now, I think you're making the wrong one."

Leo spent the following week consumed by his work, and by the week's end he was completely drained of both energy and emotion.

And he missed Mandy more than he thought he would.

Saturday morning, his father requested that Leo and Isa come to the house for brunch. After sleeping in and taking a hot shower, Leo felt rested enough to join his family. As he walked through the door, the smell of fried potatoes filled his nostrils. He walked into the kitchen and his mouth fell open. His father stood at the island, kneading dough, as Isa seasoned a pan of diced potatoes. It had been so long since Leo had seen his father even attempt to cook that the sight of his dad up to his elbows in flour made Leo's heart fill to capacity.

"Dad?" Leo said in shock. His father smiled.

"It's a good day, son."

A good day—Leo had grown to appreciate every good day Gabriel Romano had. He slipped his jacket off and moved to the sink to wash his hands.

Isa nodded toward the carton of eggs on the counter. "Mom wants scrambled eggs, Leo. Get started."

Leo grinned. Every family member had the tendency to be bossy in the kitchen, himself included.

"Has Isa told you about her boyfriend, Leo?" his dad teased.

"He's not my boyfriend, Dad!" She turned to Leo to explain. "One of the physical therapists we refer patients to asked me out to dinner."

"And you said yes?" Leo pressed.

"I told him anywhere but Romano's, now that my brother's in charge," Isa said with a giggle.

"Oh, yeah?" Leo grabbed an apron from the counter and threw it at her.

"All right, all right. More cooking, less talking," Leo's mother instructed as she entered the kitchen. She kissed Gabriel's cheek and then began to set the table, singing softly in Italian as she worked. Once the four of them were seated together, Gabriel prayed over the food.

After the teasing and laughter that always accompanied a Romano family meal faded, Gabriel grew serious.

"Leo, I've been thinking."

Leo wiped his mouth and pushed aside his plate, giving his dad his full attention.

"I think I may have been wrong to assume you wanted

both restaurants. I feel I pushed you into the second restaurant, and then I left you to shoulder the responsibility of both."

"That wasn't your choice, Dad," Leo reminded him. "You couldn't physically work anymore. It was time for you to retire."

"That is true. But…now I'm saying that maybe we should consider selling one of the restaurants. And if you want to sell the Franklin restaurant, you have my full support."

"Sell Romano's?" Isa echoed in alarm. One look from Leo's mother and Isa quieted.

"Yes," Gabriel said firmly. "It's just a business, Isa."

"No, it's not," Leo argued. And in that moment, Leo knew that he was right, that Romano's meant as much to him as he knew it meant to his father. Selling Romano's would be like letting go of his dad.

Leo's breathing restricted at the ever-present knowledge that the day to release his father was slowly coming. And his heart made the final decision: he would not let go of his father's life's work.

"It's more than that to all of us, Dad. Romano's is a part of me, too. I don't want to sell. It's been difficult—finding my footing, so to speak. But I know it will get easier. I can do this." Saying the words—defending the restaurant—brought Leo a sense of relief. He was keeping the restaurants—both of them. It was an absolute decision.

"I know you can, Leo," Gabriel said with both pride and sadness. "But you don't *have* to, son, and that's what I want you to understand."

The table fell silent. Leo saw the deep concern etched on Gabriel's face.

"I know I don't have to, Dad. But I choose to."

Gabriel took his wife's hand in his. "Are you sure about this?"

Leo didn't even have to think about it. "I'm sure. Maybe

for the first time since I assumed responsibility for the restaurants—I'm *sure*."

"Thank you, son."

Leo's mother and Isa were both wiping their eyes and sniffling. But Leo felt lighter; the weight of his ominous decision gone.

"Well." His father cleared his throat. "There's one more thing."

Even Leo's mother looked surprised. "Gabriel?" she asked.

"It may not be of any interest to anyone, but I was thinking we should make some sort of announcement that I have officially retired and Leonardo Romano is now both head chef and owner of both Romano's locations."

"Like a press statement?" Isa asked. Gabriel nodded.

"I also want a party," he said bluntly and Leo, his mother, and Isa all laughed at once.

"I'm serious!" Gabriel protested. Leo subdued his laughter.

"Okay, Dad. We'll plan a 'celebrate retirement' party. Do you want to have it here at the house?"

Gabriel shook his head. "No, we'll have it at the restaurant. Your mother and I will compose the guest list—mostly family, but there are some close friends that I'd like to include, as well. It will be a time to celebrate and reflect, to thank God for what He's done and to pray He gives you wisdom, Leo, as you take this new step."

Leo nodded. A party was an excellent idea.

"I want to have the party soon. I want to celebrate while I still feel strong enough to take part in the festivities. We all know my health is declining. Your mother and I have already discussed the need for extra help here at the house. It's time for us to really accept what's going on here and proceed accordingly."

"What do you mean, Dad?" Isa asked.

"He means that we're going to be making a few changes around here. We'll be redoing the bathrooms so that they're more accommodating for your dad. We're going to make some modifications to the kitchen, as well. We'll be having a maid come twice a week to help with the household chores," Leo's mother informed them.

"God has been so gracious to me," Gabriel said emphatically. "But though the medications have helped so far and the symptoms have been measured, I can feel things progressing. The tremors are more frequent. More days than not, I feel very weak."

The brokenness on Isa's face at their father's admission moved Leo to place an arm around her shoulders for support.

"We'll have a party whenever you want, Dad," Leo agreed.

"I'll help with the planning. I'm sure we can pull this together quickly," Isa added.

"We'll need a little time. Tony and his family will want to come from Los Angeles," Leo's mother acknowledged. "We'll look at the calendar and let you know, Leo. As for the announcement—"

"Oh, yes," Gabriel interjected. "There's someone very specific I'd like to talk with about that."

Leo raised his eyebrows. "And who is that?"

Gabriel crossed his arms, letting everyone at the table know his decision was not up for negotiation.

"Mandy Seymour."

Chapter 12

Mandy hung up the phone, still in shock over the fact that Gabriel Romano had called and asked her to be the one to announce his retirement via *Denver Lifestyle* magazine. Ann would be elated, of course. Mandy knew without a doubt that the magazine would run the story.

But to ask her now? After Leo had made the decision to cool their relationship… Mandy wondered how he was feeling about his father's decision to involve her. Would he be annoyed? Glad? *It doesn't matter. It's a privilege to be the one to do this for Gabriel, regardless of Leo.*

Sitting at her office desk, Mandy felt compelled to bow her head and pray. She could almost hear Ashley telling her to turn the entire situation over to God. And her friend would be right. In fact, Mandy felt compelled to pray about anything and everything these days.

The moment her prayer ended, a chime announced that she'd received an email. Mandy opened her inbox.

Dear Ms. Seymour,

I'm a representative of the Take Me There travel network. You might be familiar with our website and TV show. To be honest, I've enjoyed reading your column for several years.

Your recent review for Heaven-Sent B and B stood out to me, making me wonder whether you'd be interested in doing more reviews with a travel angle. Your reputation as an excellent food critic is indisputable.

We'd love to see you expand your reviews outside of the Colorado area. For example, there's a celebrity-owned restaurant opening in New York in two months—if you partnered with Take Me There, we'd love to fly you to New York and have you write a critique for us. I would be pleased to work with you on a permanent basis. Or freelance, if you prefer.

If you are at all interested, please call me at (800) 555-3491.

I look forward to hearing from you,

Bernice St. James
Representative
Take Me There

Mandy reread the email three times before even blinking. *Of course* she'd heard of Take Me There. She loved watching their reality show where travel guides visited everything from restaurants to resorts and decided whether to recommend the places.

Mandy instantly pulled up the website.

I could be a columnist for Take Me There! I could write reviews for restaurants all over the world!

Mandy's pulse raced and she was so excited she could barely breathe. The moment the clock turned five, Mandy rushed to the elevator. In her haste, she stumbled through the elevator doorway, colliding with a complete stranger.

"Hey!" the young man in a suit said, trying to right Mandy and release her hold on him.

"Oh, gosh. I'm sorry. I'm just in a hurry."

He frowned and gave her a curt nod. When the doors

opened, Mandy tried to contain her enthusiasm and move more slowly.

"By the way," the man said with a smirk. "Did you know your shirt is inside out?"

"What?" Mandy stopped in her tracks and checked her sweater.

Inside out.

She'd have to worry about it later. Mandy picked up her speed, reached her car and drove straight to Ashley's. She was sitting in the driveway, her car idling, when Ashley drove up.

"What on earth? Mandy, what's going on here?" Ashley unlocked the door to her town house and Mandy followed her in, explaining everything so quickly that she had to gasp to catch her breath.

"You're goin' a mile a minute, girl. Slow down." Ashley dropped her purse and shoulder bag on the floor and motioned for Mandy to follow her to the kitchen. "I'm glad you're here. You can help me get this place ready for Bible study in an hour."

"Sure, I can— What?" Mandy paused. Ashley snapped her head from side to side and placed her hands on her hips.

"Don't you dare pretend you forgot. The singles group is meeting here for Bible study in an hour. This was planned a month ago and you said you'd come."

"Um…I did forget but that doesn't matter. I'm here. I'll help. Now read this." Mandy pulled up the email on her phone and shoved it into Ashley's hands. As she read, Ashley's eyes grew wider and wider. She sat down on a bar stool.

"Oh, Mandy. Wow!"

Mandy nodded. "I know. I can't believe it."

"Are you going to call this woman?"

"I think I should at least talk to her, see what they're offering and find out what they would expect of me. I mean,

I'm not unhappy at *Denver Lifestyle,* but this could be an amazing opportunity."

"You'd be traveling a lot."

"I know! Seeing wonderful places, trying incredible foods, meeting new people—"

"What about Leo?"

It was Mandy's turn to place her hands on her hips. "Ashley! Leo is the one who has made it clear he's not ready for a relationship. I'm not putting my life on hold in the hope that he might change his mind eventually!"

"Okay, okay. Of course not."

Mandy's thoughts were flying but they jolted to a sudden stop. "I've got something else to tell you."

"About Leo?"

"About Gabriel." Mandy shared her news about Gabriel asking her to write an announcement for him.

"Well, now. Isn't that interesting? I was right. We haven't heard the last from Leo."

Mandy ignored Ashley's mischievous grin. "In case you weren't listening, Gabriel's the one I'm hearing from."

Ashley brushed that off with hardly an acknowledgment. "If you don't mind, pull out that vegetable tray from the fridge. Can you whip up some dip for the veggies, Miss Popular Food Expert? And did you know your sweater is inside out?"

Tuesday afternoon, Leo rubbed his temples and popped an aspirin in his mouth for the killer headache he'd been trying to ignore. He'd spent the morning talking over scheduling changes with his chefs at the Fifteenth Street restaurant. After meeting with Jeremy, whom he'd decided to name as his head chef, and Margo, Jeremy's new sous chef, he drove to the Franklin restaurant to meet with Adam and Crey and Gloria, a new addition to the team.

"So you want to keep cooking?" Adam clarified after Leo laid out his plan for a new schedule.

"At the Fifteenth Street location, yes," Leo told him. "But you've been handling the kitchen here for at least five years, Adam. I fully intend to keep that arrangement as long as it works for both of us. Of course, I'll help when needed. My father informs me that Renée has been an excellent manager for a year now. She'll continue in that role, but again, I'll be here as needed, and Renée will report to me.

"I'll be cooking only a few nights a month at the other restaurant. Jeremy will be running the kitchen the majority of the time. I'm realizing that I can't cook five nights a week and effectively be the administrator for both restaurants. I'll also be interviewing for a new manager for the Fifteenth Street location, but for now, Angelina will step in when I need more help."

The buzzing of Leo's cell phone drew his attention to the clock and he realized the meeting had run over.

"That's all for now. Thanks so much for meeting with me," Leo said, standing up and reaching out to shake hands with his chefs. Once they had left he looked down to check the missed call.

Mom.

A stab of fear came over him. He called her back immediately.

"Mom? Is everything okay?"

"Everything is fine. I just wanted to place an order to go," his mother said lightheartedly.

"Mom, we're not even open yet."

"Oh, dear. Well, then I want to invite you to dinner."

Leo chuckled and looked down at his watch. "I'm not scheduled to cook tonight, so if it's an early dinner, I can stop by for a little while."

"Would you?"

"Of course. I'll be over soon."

Afternoon traffic slowed Leo more than he had planned. But after having such positive meetings with his staff that morning, even the traffic could not dampen his mood. Leo jingled his keys in his pocket and let himself in the house, calling out to his mother that he had arrived.

He hadn't reached the kitchen, nor his parents, when there was a rap at the front door. Leo whirled back around to answer the door.

Mandy Seymour stood on the front porch, a surprised look on her face.

"Leo?"

"Mandy?"

An uncomfortable look crossed her face, and for a moment Leo felt dismayed, knowing that it was he who caused it.

"Your mother invited me for dinner. I'm supposed to meet with your father. I need to talk with him before I write the announcement."

Mom, you are unbelievable. You planned this all along.

"Oh. Come in, please." Leo held open the door as Mandy walked inside.

She didn't quite meet his eyes as she said, "I had no idea you were coming over."

He smiled, hoping to put her at ease. "I think my invitation was more of a last-minute decision on my mother's part."

"I see." The corners of her mouth turned upward. "Something smells delicious," Mandy commented. Leo recognized the scent of roast chicken. They walked together down the corridor to the kitchen. Just walking next to Mandy reminded Leo of how much he'd missed her. He wondered if it would be a bad idea to tell her so.

Probably.

As they entered the kitchen, his mother's face lit up at the sight of the two of them together.

"Mandy! I'm so happy to see you, my dear. Leonardo, your father's upstairs. Will you help him come down?"

Nice to see you, too, Mom!

Leo was clearly not the guest of honor. He obediently went upstairs, looking for his father.

"Dad?" he called out.

"I'm in the study, Leo."

Leo walked in as his father attempted to stand up, a grimace on his face. Leo rushed to his side.

"Rough day?" he asked sympathetically, reaching around his father's waist and pulling him up. His father only sighed in reply.

"I think I've been set up by Mom," Leo continued. That brought a smile to his father's face.

"Mandy's here, then."

"She is."

"Don't tell me you're disappointed by that, because I won't believe it."

Leo took slow steps, guiding his father to the top of the stairs. "No, I'm not. But it only makes things more difficult."

His dad huffed. "*You* are the one who is making things more difficult, Leonardo. We all think so. Women like Mandy Seymour don't come along every day, you know."

Leo couldn't have been annoyed even if he'd tried. The fact that Mandy was downstairs talking to his mother filled him with a happiness he'd been denying himself. For her sake, yes. But still, he wouldn't refute his father's words.

Over a plate of roast chicken and red potatoes and carrots—one of his mother's specialties—Leo joined Mandy in listening to his father share with her details of his life, his career, his accomplishments and even his illness.

Leo listened, but his gaze kept wandering to Mandy.

She's beautiful. In every way, she is absolutely beautiful.

With an inward chuckle, he remembered his initial assertion that Mandy seemed scatterbrained. Seeing her now, he realized that she was the complete opposite. He loved the easy, friendly way she interacted with his family—and everyone around her for that matter. He respected and admired her confidence in her work and her obvious capability as a successful professional. Maybe most of all, he appreciated how he felt when he was with her.

But even with all Mandy's attractive qualities, Leo knew Mandy's insecurities ran deep. He frowned.

Why can't she see herself as I see her? As God sees her?

His thoughts drifted to the night he kissed her. He had barely slept that night, distressed by how strong his feelings were, terrified of what that meant—that he could be hurt all over again.

Mandy rested her chin on the palm of her hands, completely immersed in his dad's story. Her lips curved into a full smile as his father shared with her how proud he was of Leo.

Focus, Leo. You'll never get through this night if you think of kissing her every time you look at her.

Leo helped his mother clear away the dishes and serve coffee as his father and Mandy sat talking. Mandy asked questions and jotted down pages of notes. The clock on the wall glared at Leo. He should have left hours before, but he knew he couldn't leave so he'd called in to let his staff know he couldn't make it. Angelina would keep an eye on things at the Fifteenth Street location and Renée was overseeing the Franklin restaurant. The fact that he had no idea when he might see Mandy again was enough of a reason to keep Leo where he was.

It wasn't long before his father needed rest. After helping him upstairs, Leo rejoined Mandy in the kitchen. Mandy hugged and thanked his mother, who then excused herself to help his dad.

Leo and Mandy stood awkwardly alone in the kitchen.

She doesn't want to leave, either.

"One more cup of coffee?" he asked. Mandy nodded and sat back down at the table. Leo poured two cups of coffee and sat next to her.

"Did my mother tell you about the party we're planning for my dad?"

Mandy smiled. "Yes, she invited me. I know she and Isa will be busy with the party arrangements. And I know you're busy, too—but I was wondering if there are any photos I could use for my article. I'd love to include an old photo of your dad from when the Los Angeles restaurant first opened."

Leo brightened. "That's a great idea. I'll try to find something."

"Okay, thanks."

"And if you need to talk to me…about the article, I mean, don't hesitate. I'm not too busy to help out with that. I want you to have all the information you need." Leo hoped Mandy could hear the genuineness in his words.

"Thanks, Leo. That's good to know." After a moment, she stood up, reached for her coat draped on the back of one of the kitchen chairs and slipped it on.

"How have you been?" Leo said before he could talk himself out of it. Mandy shrugged.

"Fine. I've had several reviews to write this week."

Leo stood up next to her and took her hand in his, ignoring all the warnings in his head.

"Leo, I…" Mandy looked as though she had something to tell him, but he could see her swallow her words.

"Go on," Leo pressed. She shook her head and let go of his hand. Leo desperately wanted to reach back out and hold her, but he didn't. Mandy slid her purse strap over her shoulder.

"Mandy…" Leo searched for the right words. "I hope

you know that if things were different for me…if my life looked different—"

She raised her eyebrows and waited. "It's not me, it's you, right?" she said.

Leo's shoulders slumped. It sounded so cliché and he knew it.

"Mandy, I care about you." He wanted to yell in frustration. Never before had he been so at a loss for the right words.

Leo didn't want to push her, especially now that things felt strained between them. So he just walked her to the front porch. The temperature had dropped considerably and a dusting of snow covered the ground.

"Goodnight, Leo," Mandy said. She leaned forward up on her toes and lightly kissed his cheek, then turned and walked to her car.

Chapter 13

Mandy hadn't even had a chance to take off her coat and sit down at her desk before her cell phone rang the next morning.

Leo.

All the conflicting emotions she'd felt the night before came crashing back over her. She picked up her phone.

"Hello?"

"Mandy, it's Leo. I'm sorry to bother you but I was wondering if you could come by the restaurant later today—or I could stop by your office if that would be more convenient. I stayed up late last night after you left, going through family pictures and scrapbooks. I found a box of old photos of my dad and I thought you'd like to choose one for the article."

How could she say no to that?

Mandy agreed to stop by the Fifteenth Street restaurant later that afternoon. After working on a couple of reviews and going over her schedule for upcoming reviews due within the following months, she drove to Leo's restaurant. As he'd instructed, she walked around to the back and entered through the kitchen door.

"Leo!" she called out as she set her purse on one of the kitchen counters, removed her scarf and unbuttoned her coat.

He walked into the kitchen and Mandy felt her heart tug. *Oh, Lord. Why do I have to feel this way every time I see him?*

"I've got a whole box of pictures for you to choose from," Leo explained as they walked to his office.

"Um, that's good." Mandy mentally scolded herself.

"That's good"? Stop talking, Amanda, if that's the best you can come up with.

The scolding voice in her head took on her mother's tone.

Leo pushed open the door and pointed to the photo box on his desk. Mandy reached for the picture on top of the stack. She examined the photo of a much-younger Gabriel, leaning against an old car and holding a toddler in his arms.

"You?" Mandy asked and Leo nodded. Mandy pulled up a chair and began to sort through the photographs. Leo sat next to her, pointing out details and explaining the context of the pictures when he could. Mandy loved that nearly every photo brought a smile to Leo's face.

An hour passed without Mandy noticing. She had emptied the box, spreading out the pictures across Leo's desk and studying each one. She'd found at least three good possibilities. Leo had brought Mandy a soda and warmed up a basketful of breadsticks for them to munch on as they looked at the photos together.

Mandy sipped her soda and leaned over the desk, focusing on one of her favorites, though she never would have told Leo. An old photo of Leo and Isa standing in front of a church building had caught her eye. Leo couldn't have been older than sixteen. The carefree look on his face, the easy happiness and contentment he exuded—Mandy wished she could help him feel that way again.

With a sideways glance, Mandy watched as Leo shuffled through a few photographs.

That's how he makes me feel. Happy. Content.

If only he felt the same. If only he wanted more instead of less.

Mandy sighed and tried not to feel too despondent.

A knock at the office door surprised both of them, and Angelina walked through the open door.

"Angie? Is it four already?" Leo asked, checking his watch.

Angelina smiled. "Yes. But you two finish whatever you're doing. We all know what to do in here. The kitchen's being prepped." Angelina disappeared back down the hallway.

"Have you decided, Mandy?" Leo asked.

"I'd like to use these three," Mandy said, gathering the photos and handing them to Leo. "Could you scan them and email them to me?"

Leo nodded. "Good choices," he said.

For maybe the tenth time since she'd arrived, Mandy wanted to tell Leo about her new job opportunity.

But she didn't.

"I wish we could have dinner together...." Leo's voice trailed off and he glanced at the clock on the wall. Mandy shook her head quickly, knowing he had a dinner rush to prepare for. She said a quick goodbye and drove home. Just minutes after she arrived home, the shrill sound of the Shirelles' "Mama Said" pierced the room. Mandy fell face first on her bed and held her phone up to her ear.

"Hi, Mom," she said in a muffled voice.

"Mandy? Is that you? Why are you mumbling? I haven't heard from you in days."

Some things never change.

Mandy rolled to her back and blew her hair out of her face. "I've been really busy with work, Mom."

"I see. Well, your father and I need to do some shopping

up at Park Meadows soon. We'd like you to have dinner with us. You can choose the place."

"Sure. When?"

"Saturday. Let's plan for an early dinner. Say, five. Would you want to invite Leo? Your father would like to meet him."

Mandy sat up. "I would, but I doubt he can join us. Fridays and Saturdays are his busiest evenings at the restaurant."

"Another time, then. We'll see you Saturday, Mandy."

Mandy recognized a subtle change in her mother's voice. It seemed softer somehow. Mandy also took note that she'd had a conversation with her mother and yet her blood pressure hadn't risen.

Progress. Thank you for that, Lord.

Without a doubt, Mandy knew where they would be having dinner Saturday night. And she hoped her favorite chef would be cooking.

Another email from Bernice St. James on Thursday pushed Mandy to respond, agreeing to a phone interview on Friday morning. Since Mandy often worked from home on Fridays, she knew she'd have the time and the privacy for the interview.

She'd spent Friday morning telling herself that there was no reason to be nervous. After all, Ms. St. James had sought *her* out. But when her phone rang, Mandy had to sit down to fight the jitters in her stomach. Thankfully, once the interview began, the jitters subsided and she hit her stride.

Ashley had promised to come over right after the interview. She knocked on the door just fifteen minutes after Mandy texted her. Mandy swung the door open and Ashley stood in the doorway, her eyes as wide as saucers.

"Are you Take Me There's newest employee?"

Mandy rolled her eyes and pulled Ashley inside. "Of course not, Ash. I had an interview, that's all. She asked me lots of questions and then she told me more about what they have in mind for me."

"Tell me everything," Ashley said as she made herself at home, opening the refrigerator and pulling out a carton of milk. "Do you have bagels?"

Mandy nodded and pointed to the pantry. "I want one, too."

They sat across from each other at Mandy's kitchen table, eating toasted blueberry bagels with cream cheese and drinking milk.

"It sounds good," Mandy admitted. Ashley pursed her lips.

"Tell me."

"It's a fabulous opportunity. The pay is great. The benefits are comparable to what I've got now—that's if I choose to go with them full-time. I could just freelance. Bernice would like for me to have a regular column on the website, sort of like my own blog."

"You have a regular column now," Ashley pointed out. Mandy nodded.

"That's true. But *Denver Lifestyle* is all about Colorado. With Take Me There, I'd be traveling all over the country and even internationally! They'd be paying me to travel! If the blog really took off, they'd consider doing TV specials for their network. Can you believe that, Ash? A film crew would follow me as I explore resorts and restaurants all over the world!"

Ashley smiled. "That does sound amazing."

"I know!" Mandy's excitement bubbled over. "I mean, don't you think I should take it?"

Ashley looked thoughtful. "I think you should pray about it. And if God gives you the green light, then go for it, absolutely. Dive in headfirst. But if you feel any hesitation, wait."

Mandy nodded her agreement. "Of course, I mean, I'm definitely going to pray about this before I make a final decision. Bernice is going to email me the official offer so I have time to think it all through. I know what you're thinking, Ashley."

"Do tell."

"*What about Leo?* You're wondering whether I'd be up for this job if he wanted to pursue a relationship with me right now."

"Well, would you?"

Mandy shrugged. "I don't know. And it doesn't matter because Leo has told me frankly that he's not looking for a relationship right now."

"And you believe him?"

Not really.

"All I can go on is what he told me."

"Do you want to know what I think?" Ashley asked. Mandy pretended to think it over.

"Well…"

Ashley didn't blink. "I think you've fallen in love with Leonardo Romano."

Mandy kept her eyes diverted. "Even if that were true, it's not enough, Ashley."

"Not enough? Since when is love not enough?"

Mandy looked up. "It's never enough when it's one-sided. He has to decide whether he wants to pursue *me.* He has to decide whether he's in love with *me.*"

"And if he does just that?" Ashley pondered aloud.

Mandy looked down.

"Then…I don't know."

"Let me point out one thing, Mandy. Traveling to all those wonderful, romantic resorts, dining at all those incredible restaurants—it might be a little lonely when you're always asking for a table for one."

"Well, that's my only option right now, Ashley," Mandy replied, hurt seeping into her words. Ashley grasped Mandy's hand.

"There's another option, honey. It's called faith."

Chapter 14

Two days passed and Leo wondered whether the energy he spent *not* calling Mandy was worth the effort.

Saturday evening Leo sighed with relief that he wasn't scheduled to cook. He did plan to divide up his time between both restaurants, overseeing the staff. After a quick run-through of the Franklin restaurant, Leo made his way to the Fifteenth Street location. He got caught up responding to emails in his office when a flustered Angelina knocked twice and then opened the door before he could even speak.

"Angie, what's wrong?"

"One of the servers called in sick so I was helping out, but tonight is supposed to be my first night running the hostess station. Can you call Dana and see if she's available? Or maybe someone from Franklin can come over."

Leo was already flipping through his scheduling book as he waved Angelina back.

"I'll call. You hostess."

She ducked out and then whirled back around.

"Leo, you *are* planning to stop by and at least say hi, right?"

He didn't look up. "I'll do a walk-through later and speak to customers."

"What if she's not here by that point?"

Leo stopped what he was doing and looked up. "Angelina, what are you talking about?"

"Mandy's here with her parents. Table eighteen. They've already ordered." With that, Angelina's hair swished behind her as she walked away.

Leo sat frozen for a moment before remembering that he needed to find another server. After being reassured that Dana could be there within half an hour, he hung up the phone and gave himself a minute to compose himself before heading straight to table eighteen.

Angelina had seated Mandy and her parents at a table near where he and Mandy had shared dessert. Flashes from that night crossed his mind—Mandy's wavy hair, her notepad on the table, the inviting smile that was reflected in her eyes, the adorable freckles on her face.

"Mandy," he said as he approached the table. He tried to decipher the look on her face. Relief? Had she been waiting for him? Hoping to see him?

The fact alone that she chose his restaurant answered that question for him. Mandy introduced Leo to her father, whose warm handshake and friendly smile put Leo further at ease. Leo was quick to tell Mandy's mother how glad he was to see her again.

"Can you join us for a few minutes?" Mandy asked. Even if he had been working in the kitchen, the hopeful tone in her voice would have been enough for him to face chaos rather than say no. As it was, he slid into the booth next to Mandy.

"I would love to join you. I'm not cooking tonight."

"Oh, dear. And we've heard so much about your Lobster Magnifico!" Mandy's father joked. Leo enjoyed the light flush that crept up on Mandy's cheeks.

"I can assure you that our chef tonight will do an excellent job," Leo said, nodding at their server, Kelly, when she held up a pitcher of water. She brought Leo a glass of water, behind her was a server in training, carrying the family's order.

"Would you like anything, chef?" Kelly asked as they distributed the plates.

"Just water, thanks."

"You never told me, Leo, is the Lobster Magnifico one of your creations? Or is it a family recipe?" Mandy asked.

He was very aware that they were sitting so close in the booth that Mandy's shoulder was pressed up against his.

"It's mine, actually. It was a dish I created for a class when I was in culinary school. It was part of my end-of-the-year exam. We were all charged with coming up with something new, and we were graded on taste, appearance, and creativity."

"You created that for a grade?" Mandy reiterated, surprise evident in her voice.

"I did." He didn't want to brag and tell them that he'd been given a perfect score—the only one in the class.

"Well, I hope you received an A." Mandy grinned.

Leo just nodded nonchalantly. "As a matter of fact, not long after opening this restaurant, one of my old professors asked if he could bring in his new class. They crowded into the kitchen to watch me make the sauce."

"So you're the kind of chef who shares his recipes?" Mandy's father said.

Leo chuckled. "Not exactly. But that professor already had the recipe since I'd been required to turn it in for the class. And out of respect for me, he had every student sign an agreement not to duplicate my recipe for the public. To be honest, there are several old family recipes that we want to keep just within our family. And while many of our dishes are common Italian foods, my father spent years experimenting with different spices and sauces to make his version of those meals unique in some way. I do the same thing. And we usually keep those additions to our recipes

out of the public knowledge. We have what we call our Romano family cookbook, where my father writes down his
recipes—some of which are not used in our restaurants.
Many were derived from his time spent in Italy, given to
him by my great-grandmother."

"Mandy told us about your father's illness, Leo. That
must be difficult for you. How is he?" Mandy's mother
asked delicately. Leo's throat constricted.

"He's…struggling. We were lucky that for a long time,
his symptoms were almost nonexistent. But over the past
few months things have progressed. Still, he's a man of
faith. I think I'm learning as much from him now as I did
growing up."

The truth in his own words struck Leo.

He felt weak with sadness at that moment and he hated
it. Without thinking, he reached for Mandy's hand beneath
the table. She held his hand tightly, and her immediate response strengthened him.

She makes me stronger. She helps me.

Leo could hear his mother's words to him, implying
that Mandy could be God's gift to help him through this
hard time.

"So what do you think about Mandy's new job offer,
Leo?" her father asked.

Mandy paled and dropped Leo's hand. "I haven't mentioned it to Leo yet, Dad. We're not…"

"What job offer?" Leo interrupted, hoping to keep
Mandy from explaining that they were supposedly just
friends and therefore she wasn't obligated to tell him such
important news as a job offer.

Even though the thought bothered him.

*We were together all afternoon on Wednesday. Why
didn't she tell me?*

"Um, well…you've probably never heard of the network
Take Me There—" Mandy began.

"I've heard of it," Leo said curtly.

"Oh. Well, I've been offered a job as a columnist. I'd have a regular feature on the website. I would be doing reviews for restaurants all over the country, maybe even in other countries. I'd also be reviewing resorts and hotels and that type of thing."

"And Mandy would be on TV!" her mother exclaimed with a glowing smile.

Mandy looked embarrassed. "That's only a possibility. It would depend on how the readership responded to my articles."

"That sounds like a lot of travel," Leo said in what he hoped was an even-toned, just-curious voice. Mandy sipped her water and then nodded.

"Yes, it would be. I haven't decided whether to take the job or not," she said, her eyes safely on the dish in front of her.

Leo knew his ill-temper was irrational. He'd told Mandy he couldn't pursue a relationship with her. Why, then, did he feel so angry that she wouldn't tell him about a new job opportunity? More than that, why did he feel so desperate at the thought of her taking a job that would take her even farther away from him?

He inhaled and mustered all the composure he could. "Well, that sounds like an incredible opportunity for you, Mandy. Congratulations."

"Thank you, Leo." Mandy didn't even look at him.

They were both silent. Leo could feel Mandy's parents looking from him to Mandy and back to him.

"I need to go check on the kitchen staff," Leo said finally. "It was so nice to meet you, Mr. Seymour. Claire, it was a pleasure." Leo stood up. "Mandy," his voice faltered.

The rigidness in her face spoke volumes.

What does she want from me?

For a moment their eyes met and they just looked at each other in silence.

What do I want from her? I'm purposely holding back... but I don't want her to do the same. It's not fair. I know it's not.

Mandy forced a fake smile. "It was nice to see you, Leo."

He wondered how those words could sound so sad.

Mandy appreciated her mom's light chatter on the way back to her apartment. She hated that the evening had ended so awkwardly and the last thing she wanted to do was talk about it with both of her parents.

Taking Mom and Dad to Romano's was a terrible idea. What was I thinking? Leo tells me he doesn't want a relationship with me, and yet I still decide to take my parents to his restaurant, hoping to see him? I'm pathetic.

When they reached her home, Mandy's parents came inside for coffee. Knowing her mother would be visiting, Mandy had cleaned her apartment from top to bottom. She turned on her coffeemaker as her father flipped through the television channels and her mother joined her in the kitchen, trying to inconspicuously find something to clean.

"I'm sorry that your father brought up the job, Mandy. We didn't realize you hadn't told Leo yet," her mother said as she opened a cabinet and began straightening pots and pans.

Mandy shrugged. "It's okay. He's not my boyfriend or anything. It's not a big deal."

Her mother turned around and gave her a look that told Mandy she didn't believe a word she said.

"I'm serious! He's too busy right now for a relationship. We're just friends."

"He paid for our meal tonight, Mandy," her mother reminded her. Mandy stared at the coffeepot.

"He's that kind of friend."

"What kind is that?"

"The considerate and generous kind," Mandy said brusquely. She pulled spoons out of the drawer and set the sugar bowl on the table.

"Well, he seemed miffed that you hadn't told him about the job," her mother pointed out. "That seems like a reaction from someone who wants to be more than friends."

I know.

"Even so, I told you, he's made it really clear that he's not looking for a romantic relationship right now. So that's that." Mandy pulled a carton of creamer out of the refrigerator.

Her mother touched her arm.

"Mandy, he drove to Evergreen to cook you dinner."

"To cook *us* dinner," Mandy corrected as she got out three mugs.

"You might not be able to see it, but from where I was sitting tonight, I would say that Leo Romano is crazy about you."

Mandy's heart pounded like a drum and she looked at her mom.

"What makes you say that?"

Her mother smiled. "Oh, the way he looked at you. The way every time you moved, he noticed. The way his entire demeanor changed at the possibility of you traveling all over the world. The chemistry between you two was probably only surpassed by the tension after he heard about your job offer. You need to talk to him."

Mandy sighed and sank into one of the kitchen chairs. "I do. I mean, I want to. But at this point, I'm waiting for Leo. If he wants to be more than friends, he's going to have to make that clear to me."

Claire sat next to her. "What are you going to do about the job?"

The sound of the coffeemaker clicking off caused Mandy to stand up, pull out the coffeepot and fill the three cups.

She took her time answering. When she did, she tried to sound more positive than she felt.

"Mom, I think I'm going to take it. It's a great job. An incredible opportunity. I've always wanted to travel, see new places, experience new things, try exotic foods."

Her mother nodded. "I see. Would you say it's your dream job?"

Mandy poured cream into her coffee and then stirred in two spoonfuls of sugar. "In some ways, I guess."

"What do you mean?" her mom asked.

What do *I mean? What am I trying to say?*

"Sometimes dreams change," Mandy said quietly.

Understanding filled her mother's eyes. "Yes. Sometimes they do."

Chapter 15

Ree Drummond's voice filled the room from the television. Mandy had just watched "the Pioneer Woman" cook pork chops with pineapple fried rice, her stomach growling at the very thought of it. During a commercial break, Mandy picked up the invitation on her coffee table and looked at it for maybe the tenth time. "You are invited to a reception in honor of Gabriel Romano."

Mandy sighed. Of course, she would go. She wouldn't think of missing Gabriel's party, but the idea of seeing Leo caused a swarm of butterflies to rush through her stomach. They hadn't spoken since the semi-disastrous dinner at his restaurant more than a week ago. The disappointment settled into Mandy all over again.

It was my fault.

But why did he get so angry about the job offer? Is he annoyed because I didn't tell him earlier? Is he frustrated with the idea of me being gone all the time? What's his problem?

Those questions played on repeat in Mandy's thoughts, but she wasn't about to actually voice them to Leo. Mandy felt certain it was Leo's turn to make a move, if he were so inclined.

I feel like I'm playing a game of cat and mouse. Unfortunately, I don't know whether I'm the cat or the mouse.

Mandy muted the television, unable to concentrate. She kicked her feet up on the coffee table and rested her head back on the sofa as she stared at the ceiling. Ms. Bernice St. James wanted an answer and Mandy didn't have one for her yet.

While the thought of traveling to new places enticed her, Mandy knew that even though she enjoyed a nice vacation every now and then, traveling usually exhausted her. What would it be like to constantly go from airport to airport, stay in hotel after hotel, live out of a suitcase and leave her family and friends behind?

Ashley was right—always asking for a table for one gets old fast. Still, it's the opportunity of a lifetime. God, is this from you? Is this the right direction for my life? What about Leo?

Mandy loved her job at *Denver Lifestyle,* but she'd always been open to the idea of leaving if something better came along. And wasn't this offer from Take Me There better?

A heavy feeling pressed on her heart.

It's a great offer. It's just not the one I want.

Leo passed a bowl of salad to Angelina and accepted the plate of ricotta gnocchi that one of the waiters handed him. Once every quarter, Leo's father served a staff dinner before opening. Leo intended to do the same. They'd pushed together tables at the back of the Fifteenth Street restaurant and enjoyed a family-style dinner of salad, bread and ricotta gnocchi. Leo listened idly to the conversation around him, but his thoughts kept going to Mandy and the awkward way things had ended between them the night she and her parents came to the restaurant.

Every time he thought about his reaction to the news about her job offer—in front of her parents, no less—he wanted to groan. He wished he'd held back his frustration for a time when he could have talked privately with

Mandy. Even then, she had every right to take any job she wanted, and since he'd decided not to pursue a relationship with her right now, of course she wouldn't feel obligated to tell him about it.

Everything about the situation felt wrong and Leo hated it. He wanted to be in a relationship with Mandy. The idea of her traveling for weeks out of the year didn't thrill him, but even if she did take the job, he wanted, at the very least, for her to discuss it with him.

Still, going back to her now and telling her he'd changed his mind seemed immature and indecisive. His situation hadn't changed. Well, not much. Accepting the reality that he wanted to keep the restaurants—and feeling at peace with it—had made a difference. Delegating more of his responsibilities had lessened his burden, as well. His father's illness, however, was a different matter. Leo just didn't see how he could both accept that and have peace about it.

"How's Mandy, chef?" Leo heard Angelina ask quietly, interrupting his reverie.

"She's fine, I guess."

Angelina reached across the table for a pitcher of iced tea and refilled both their glasses. "Leo, you know, the family really liked her."

"*I* really like her. It's just not good timing," he said in a voice that he hoped communicated his desire to talk about something else.

"For you, cousin, the timing will probably never be ideal," she said matter-of-factly. Leo looked over at her.

"What do you mean?"

She gave an easy shrug. "Leo! You know restaurant life better than anyone else. There's always going to be stress. Your schedule will always be a little unpredictable."

"That's true to an extent," Leo agreed.

"To more than an extent," Angelina insisted. "What there will *not* always be is a Mandy Seymour in front of you."

Leo swallowed hard. "I know. But right now, my dad…"

Angelina cut him off. "Your dad's situation is something our family will continue to deal with. We'll trust God. You are *not* in this alone or shouldering the sole responsibility for your dad's health. We'll all help take care of him for as long as he needs help. That's what our family does, Leo. You *know* this. A few years from now, another family member might become ill. Will you continue to put your life on hold because of these things?"

That thought hadn't occurred to him.

"I don't know, Angelina!" Leo's temper flared. Rather than back down, Angelina narrowed her eyes and kept her voice even.

"Well, you'd better figure it out. You should take a lesson from your father, Leo. Do you know why Uncle Gabriel has been so successful? The restaurants alone would never have been enough to make him happy. It was you and Isa and Aunt Rosalinda who made him successful. It was his faith that made him strong."

"He wasn't always strong," Leo said, almost to himself. He thought of the many nights his father had come home well after midnight, exhausted. The times when finances were strained and his father's brow was creased with worry.

"Leo," Angelina's voice softened. "Don't you see? He wasn't strong on his own."

Leo didn't answer but Angelina's words reached their mark.

"I think, perhaps, you're trying to be strong on your own. That won't work, Leo. You need your faith in God to sustain you. You need your family, all of us, to support you. And just maybe, you need Mandy Seymour to love you."

Leo pushed Angelina's words to the back of his mind as he cooked that evening, but they kept creeping up, inconveniencing him as he tried to work. The thought that

Mandy and he were a good match had occurred to him several times. But the notion that he *needed* her, that she just might be the one person God intended for him, that she could make all the difference in his life… Leo couldn't entertain those thoughts. Not when he'd pushed her away. The sound of a tray crashing caused Leo to wince.

"What happened?" he barked out. Kelly rushed over to help one of the other servers who looked near to tears.

"An accident, chef," she said. "Okay, we need another plate of crab-stuffed ravioli, guys. And an order of chicken marsala. And we need it now!"

Leo bit his tongue to keep from yelling out that he couldn't handle any more accidents. He turned back to the stack of orders in front of him and zeroed in on what he needed to do next. In his pocket, Leo's cell phone buzzed. He closed his eyes, the stack of orders looming over him, his neck aching from stiffness. He pulled out his phone and answered it.

"Isa?"

"Leo, can you come over to Mom and Dad's?"

The eerie calm in Isa's voice caused him to freeze. "What happened?"

"Dad's okay. He's just…confused."

"Should you just take him to the hospital and I'll meet you there?"

"I've tried. He won't get in the car. Can you come?"

Leo took a deep breath and exhaled, trying not to let the anxiety he already felt choke him.

"I've got a couple more orders to finish and then I think Jeremy can handle it. Is it urgent or can I come in half an hour?"

"Just come as soon as you can. I'll try to keep things under control until then."

Forty-five minutes later, Leo was ushering his dad into his car. He understood what had Isa worried. Their dad was confused about where he was. He seemed frustrated and angry. But after a lot of gentle coaxing, Leo managed to get him in the car.

It was a new kind of fear for Leo.

He talked calmly to his dad on the way; Isa and Rosalinda had followed behind them. The confusion seemed to make his father even more upset. Isa had called the hospital before they arrived. Dr. Rosas was unavailable so they would see the on-call doctor.

They made it to the hospital and Leo stayed with his mother to help check Gabriel in while Isa went with their dad and the nurse. Rosalinda finished the paperwork and Leo walked with her to his dad's hospital room. Leo tried to exude a calm and steady presence at the sight of his mother's fearful eyes. She leaned into him, holding his arm. After Dr. Andrews saw Gabriel, he spoke with Leo, Rosalinda and Isa.

"I think it's a combination of things. He's exhausted from lack of sleep. Insomnia is common in Parkinson's patients. He also seems to be somewhat depressed. Mind you, I've seen patients who are severely depressed, and Gabriel doesn't fit that pattern. But he is frustrated with his circumstances and fatigued. We need to consider medication for anxiety. His blood pressure is low again, so I will monitor that overnight. I'll let him rest for now and come back and check on him later."

"Thank you, Doctor," Leo said as Dr. Andrews left the room. Then the three of them moved to surround his father's bed. Leo could tell from his father's droopy eyes that his dad was exhausted. He patted his leg.

"You're going to be all right, Dad. Rest. We'll be here when you wake up."

His father nodded and closed his eyes.

Leo left to find a waiting room. He wanted to call Mandy. It had been nearly two weeks since he'd seen her, but he knew she'd want to hear about his dad's health. And in truth, he needed her to know. He turned a corner and froze at the sight of her walking down the corridor.

"Mandy?"

Mandy's face was filled with concern. "Isa texted me. What happened?"

Leo was so relieved to see her. The waiting room was only a few steps away so they made their way to one of the sofas. Leo sat down, feeling depleted from the rush of emotions. "He was confused and angry. He couldn't seem to remember why Mom had moved some furniture around. He was snapping at my mother and Isa, which is unusual for him. So we came in. They're going to give him medication to help with anxiety."

Leo took a ragged breath. "He's getting worse. He's getting weaker. He's…"

Mandy moved closer to Leo, wrapping her arms around him. He buried his face in her neck, trying not to cry.

Mandy held her breath as Leo tightened his arms around her.

"I'm here, Leo," she said soothingly.

She felt empty when he finally released her and sat back. He was hurting and there was nothing she could do.

He took her hand and pulled her up with him.

Mandy hesitated. "Leo, you go on without me. I know you need to be with your family right now. Why don't I go get some coffee for Isa and your mom? Would they like that?"

He didn't let go of her hand. "My dad adores you, Mandy. He won't mind that you're here."

The words touched Mandy's heart, but he didn't quite say what she needed to hear.

What about you, Leo? Do you adore me? Do you want me here?

Of course, she was glad that Isa had thought to text her. But would Leo have? Would he have shared this with her?

She didn't feel like she could ask. Not at this moment when Leo looked so far beyond stressed. She just let him lead her into the hospital room. Rosalinda immediately crossed the room and hugged her.

"Thank you for coming, Mandy," she said warmly. Mandy hugged her back, feeling out of place yet thankful to be included. Isa reached for her next.

"Thanks for texting me," Mandy whispered. Isa leaned close to Mandy's ear.

"You're family, Mandy. Leo's always the last to know these things."

After spending a couple of hours at the hospital, eating dinner from Styrofoam boxes and watching TV in Gabriel's hospital room, Leo walked Mandy out to the parking lot.

"Will you stay the night?" Mandy asked.

"Yes. Isa's working tonight." He still held her hand loosely as they walked. "Thank you for being here," he said.

Mandy shook her head. "You don't have to thank me, Leo. I care about your family. I want to be here for all of you."

He looked down and Mandy waited, hoping he'd say something, anything. She wanted to take him in her arms and hold him and comfort him. She also wanted to yell at him for pushing her away.

"Are you taking the job?" he asked. Mandy blinked.

Really? You want to bring this up now?

"I'm not sure, Leo. I'm praying about it."

He looked at her with bloodshot eyes, exhausted, stressed.

It was not the right time to have this discussion.

"Why didn't you tell me before? We spent so much time together that Wednesday, but you didn't tell me about the job opportunity."

Mandy didn't respond for a moment. "I'm not sure why I didn't tell you that day when we were looking at all the photos. I really wanted to."

"You didn't have to," Leo admitted.

"I know," Mandy agreed. "The fact that I didn't tell you, is that why you seemed upset that night at the restaurant?"

"It frustrated me. And then the realization that you might be traveling all the time just…I don't know. It's hard to explain."

No, it's not.

They were both quiet.

"You made the decision not to be in a relationship with me, Leo," Mandy tried to sound stronger than she felt at that moment. "I have to make decisions based on what's best for me."

He nodded, not quite making eye contact. "I know. But…I still wish you had told me."

Mandy hated that they were having this conversation.

"What would you have said?" she asked, trying to keep the edge out of her voice.

He sighed. "I don't know."

Mandy felt a wave of impatience rush through her. "It's been a really long evening. Let's talk about this another time," she said.

"You see the stress I'm under, Mandy. You know it's not that I don't want to be in a relationship with you. It's that I can't."

"I'm not asking for that, Leo. Especially since you keep so kindly reminding me that you're unable to be in a relationship." Mandy bit her lip.

You're at the hospital! Give the guy a break.

Leo closed his eyes, shook his head and exhaled, obviously annoyed.

"Can you tell me whether you're leaning toward accepting the job offer?" he asked.

Mandy didn't even try to mask her exasperation. *"Leo."*

"I need to know, Mandy. I know I'm not your boyfriend, and I know you don't have to tell me anything, but please, tell me."

"Fine. Yes, I'm leaning toward taking the job," she answered. Leo looked at her, his expression almost wounded, but he only nodded. Mandy felt a lump in her throat.

"This isn't fair to me, Leo."

"I know. I'm sorry," he said. "I don't know what to do. There's too much… I'm not handling everything very well."

"You don't have to 'handle' me. I'm just here as your friend, Leo," Mandy said, hoping the hurt in her words wasn't coming across as fiercely as it felt.

Leo looked at her. "I want more than friendship from you, Mandy."

She shook her head, her emotions flooding her. "Leo, I can't hear this. You say you can't be in a relationship with me, and then you say you want to be more than friends. I feel like a yo-yo!"

He stepped closer to her but Mandy backed away. "I need to go."

"Mandy, I'm begging you. Please try to understand."

"I do!" Mandy cried out. "I do understand. I see your life. I see what you're going through. But you're the one who won't let me in."

Leo stared at her for a moment. The silence and darkness of the parking lot surrounded them.

"She promised me everything. Her whole world. And then she walked away." His words were raw and broken.

Mandy could barely breathe. Finally she said, "I'm not Carol Ann, Leo."

"I know. Mandy, to me, you are so much more than she could ever be."

Then choose me. Choose us. Let me in.

Leo looked down and wiped his eyes. Mandy paused,

overcome by the sight of him crying. It hit her that maybe
Leo needed more than she could give.

*Father, he's so overwhelmed right now. He needs Your
peace. He needs Your strength.*

Neither of them spoke, and Mandy finally pulled out her
car keys and left.

Chapter 16

Two days had passed since the emotional showdown with Leo when Mandy drove out to Evergreen. "I'm here!" Mandy yelled, walking through her parents' home. "Mom?" she called out.

"Upstairs!" her mother responded.

"Of course," Mandy muttered, climbing the stairs.

"All right, Mom," Mandy said, walking into her parents' bedroom. "What is it you just *have* to tell me?" She stopped short, her eyes widening at the mound of suitcases piled on the bed.

"What do you think?" her mother asked, twirling around in a black dress.

"Um, where should I start?" Mandy queried. "What's going on here?"

Her mom laughed. "I'm packing. I wanted you to be the first to know. Your father and I are going on a two-week Alaskan cruise. Doesn't that sound exciting? I bought this dress because apparently there are formal dinners on the ship."

"Wow! When are you leaving?"

"In a little over two months."

Mandy motioned to the suitcases. "And you're packing now?"

"I certainly don't want to leave everything for the last minute, Amanda. Plus, I have to take inventory and see what we need to buy for the trip. For example, your father hasn't bought a new suit in more than a decade. If I'm going to be seen with him at a formal dinner, that has to be addressed."

Mandy's smile went ear to ear. "You're going on an adventure!"

Her mom nodded. "The first of many, I hope." Claire stepped toward Mandy and hugged her closely. "And I have you to thank for it. You reminded me that I'm not too old for adventure, for fun, for new experiences. You inspired me, Mandy."

Mandy could hardly speak.

Her mom twirled again in her black dress and then disappeared into her closet.

"What did you decide about the job? Did you take it?" her mother called out from the closet. Mandy began folding the pile of her father's shirts and stacking them on the bed.

"It's not official yet, but I'm planning to take it."

Her mom emerged from the closet with two pairs of shoes. "Are you sure?"

Mandy pushed aside one of the suitcases and sat down. "I think so."

Her mom leaned against the closet door frame and tilted her head.

"Are you happy, Mandy?"

Mandy nodded, but it didn't feel completely true.

I'd be a lot happier if Leonardo Romano took me in his arms and professed his undying love for me.

"What about you, Mom? Are you happy? You look happy."

Her mom looked at the jumble of clothes and luggage and smiled. "I feel blessed." She moved to the bed, kicking rolls of socks out of the way as she did so, and sat down on a pile of shirts, her gaze fixed on Mandy. "I've wasted a lot of time, Mandy, allowing discontent to bother my heart."

Mandy listened intently. "Do you want to know something, Mom? I have, too. Not discontent, necessarily, but insecurity and self-doubt. I allowed those feelings to take root. But I'm letting them go. I don't want to live under the shadow of those things anymore. They don't belong in my life."

A look of relief crossed her mother's face. "I'm letting go of my discontent, too. It has no place in my future. And I want you to know, Mandy, that I support your decisions. Whatever you decide to do about your job—I support you. Whatever happens with Leo—I support you. You don't need my approval for anything, of course," her mother said.

"But I do," Mandy contradicted. "Well, maybe I don't need it, but I want it, Mom. I've always wanted it."

To Mandy, the happiness and pride in her mother's eyes spilled over and engulfed the space around them. Her mom wrapped her arms around Mandy. And for the first time in as long as Mandy could remember, she relaxed in her mother's arms, laying her head on her shoulder and allowing herself to be loved.

Leo hated the way he'd left things with Mandy. He wanted to erase that conversation they'd had in the hospital parking lot. Every time he thought about it, he wished he hadn't brought up Carol Ann. He needed to somehow apologize without giving the impression that things could be different. After a week of texting and calling Mandy with the most minimal of responses, Leo decided to take a different approach. Armed with a brown bag holding a ham-and-cheese croissant from Myra's Coffee House, along with a regular coffee—one creamer, two sweeteners—Leo stopped by the *Denver Lifestyle* offices. The administrative assistant led him to Mandy's office.

He set the coffee and brown bag on her desk. "Peace offering?" he asked.

Mandy looked shocked at the sight of him. She recovered quickly and peeked into the bag.

"Nice choice. Thank you."

Leo nodded, standing in front of her, unsure of what to say.

"Leo," Mandy began softly. "Why are you here?"

He sat down in one of the chairs across from her. "Because I'm sorry for that night at the hospital. You were there to support me and I brought up things I should have just let go."

Mandy picked up her coffee cup. "It's okay." She looked down for a moment and then shook her head. "Actually, it's not. I mean, everything you said was fine. I want you to tell me what you're thinking and feeling. But you can't keep doing this to me. I can't take the emotional seesaw. I like you, Leo."

Leo felt his heart tug at the sound of her words.

"But I can just be your friend if you need that right now."

Just my friend.

"Is that what you want from me?" Mandy asked, her voice guarded.

No.

Leo knew she was right. He couldn't keep going back and forth with her. It wasn't fair.

He didn't answer so she kept talking. "You have to decide, Leo. If we're just going to be friends, then stop making me feel like you want more than that."

Father, what do I say right now?

"I'm sorry, Mandy. I've been unfair to you. I want you in my life, even if right now it's just as my friend."

He could see her dissatisfaction, but she took a deep breath and nodded. "Okay." He could see that there was more she needed to say. He waited silently.

"Leo, we've talked about how I've struggled with insecurity for a long time. But I've made a decision to let that go. It's time for that to change in my life."

Leo wanted to reach out and pull her to him. But he just leaned over and rested his elbows on his knees, listening to her. He realized that rather than instilling confidence in Mandy, he'd been confusing her. Maybe even making her feel less secure. The thought was disheartening.

Mandy hugged her arms to her chest. "I'm going to call the people at Take Me There and accept the job."

Leo nodded.

"Say *something*," Mandy insisted. Leo reached over and took Mandy's hand.

"If you can be my friend, I can be yours, Mandy. You will do a great job and I'm proud of you." He kissed her hand and willed his words to be true.

Two days before the party for his dad, Leo climbed the stairs at his parents' home. He'd spent the day helping his mother and Isa with last-minute preparations. It was late afternoon when he found his mother in the study, her laptop in front of her.

"What's going on?" Leo asked. His mother looked up, wiping a tear from her eyes.

"Mandy's announcement was posted today, Leo," she said.

Today?

"Sit here, son," his mother said, standing up from her seat. "Read this," she told him before leaving the room.

How do you measure a man's life? Is it in dollars and cents and buildings and awards? For myself, I don't think so. I have the privilege of sharing with you the news that the great chef Gabriel Romano is hanging up his hat and taking a much-deserved retirement.

Over the past few weeks, I've spent time with Gabriel and his family, and he's given me a glimpse into his life. Like me, you may know him as the owner of award-winning restaurants, as a successful entrepreneur and as a generous philanthropist.

But here's what I've discovered about Gabriel Romano: He's real. He's the type of man who, at the age of twenty-one, married the love of his life and told her this on their wedding day: "There are many dreams and goals in my heart. But no matter where this life takes us or what I endeavor to do, remember this—all of my dreams and goals begin and end with you."

He's the type of man who started a restaurant with nothing more than a hope and a prayer. His children grew up playing in their father's kitchen. It was his dedication and perseverance that turned Romano's into a name associated with respect, quality and success. But it was more than just dedication and perseverance—Mr. Romano is a man of faith, whose life is a picture of belief, hope, truth and love.

Gabriel Romano has given me permission to share with you that he has been diagnosed with Parkinson's disease. His family is surrounding him with love and support at this time. At Mr. Romano's request, his son, Leo, has assumed responsibility of both Romano's establishments in Denver.

Leonardo Romano is much like his father. It seems that he, too, has been blessed with the innate culinary sense that his father was given. As a chef, the younger Romano has the creative genius that made Gabriel Romano's dishes so unique and flavorful. But it pleases me more to say that Leonardo Romano has his father's work ethic, compassion and integrity. As

Gabriel Romano said to me, "Romano's is in good hands." I believe him.

Thank you, Mr. Romano, for all the years you've given us.

Leo exhaled, undone by Mandy's words.

"It's a beautiful tribute." Leo turned around, shocked to hear his father's voice. He stood in the doorway, holding a cane. Leo jumped up.

"Dad! Shouldn't you be lying down?"

"I'm all right, Leo. The new medication is helping today. The doctor said I should be moving around, within reason." Leo helped his father sit in the leather chair by the window.

"How do you do it, Dad? How do you keep trusting, keep holding on to hope, keep believing?"

His dad looked at him with concern. "Don't you understand, Leo? I *can't* do those things on my own. Neither can you, son. And you don't have to, so stop trying."

I will never leave you nor forsake you.

Leo recognized the familiar voice in his head, the one voice that could reassure him when everything seemed bleak. The one that kept coming back even when he tried not to listen.

Come to me, all you who are weary and burdened.

Unable to speak, Leo bowed his head for a moment. The stress he was under was suffocating him. He couldn't handle it. Something had to give.

God...help me to trust You through this.

He felt a peace rush over him and he wondered why he'd fought it so long. He recognized the feeling of acceptance, of giving in, and he welcomed it.

"I don't understand all of this, Dad. But...I think I have to trust that God does."

"Sometimes, Leo," his father said, his voice soft and weary, "that's all we can do."

Mandy inundated Leo's thoughts all over again. Hadn't she told him the very same thing? Leo knew instinctively that both she and his father spoke the truth. And that God had intentionally placed both of them in his life.

Leo looked back at his father. "Dad, what do you think of Mandy?"

His dad smiled. "I think she's the one for you, Leo. But more importantly, what do *you* think of her?"

Leo looked back at the article on the computer screen. He could almost hear Mandy saying the heartfelt words directly to him. It was right there, clear as day—how she felt about him.

"I know she's the one for me," he said, more to himself than to his Dad.

Now he just had to take back all the nonsense he'd told her. He needed to convince Mandy Seymour that she could trust him with her heart—and that his heart already belonged to her.

Chapter 17

Mandy honked her horn twice. The door to Ashley's town-home opened, but all Mandy could see was Ashley's hand reaching out, giving her a "hold on!" gesture, and then disappearing back inside. Mandy sat back in annoyance and checked the clock again.

We're going to be late.

At the last minute that Sunday evening, Mandy had decided to force Ashley to be her plus-one at Gabriel Romano's retirement party. Going with Ashley sounded better than showing up alone. At least it *had,* until Ashley proceeded to make them both late. The front door finally opened and Ashley dashed out to the car.

"Ash—" Mandy began as Ashley slid into the passenger seat and slammed the door.

"Waitin' on you now, honey. Let's get this show on the road."

"Grrr!" Mandy said loudly in vexation, and Ashley chuckled.

"All right, I'm sorry it took me a little longer than I thought to get ready. You're taking me to a restaurant that will be teeming with Italian men. I obviously need to look my best."

"You're there to be my wingman, not to find an Italian husband."

"You obviously don't understand the concept of a wingman, or wingwoman."

"Ashley!"

"You're right. Let's drop it."

Mandy found a parking spot in the last row in the lot.

"Looks like a good turnout," Ashley said cheerfully as they walked together toward the entrance of the Franklin Romano's. Liz held the door open as they approached.

"Mandy!" she exclaimed with a grin.

"Hi, Liz." Mandy reached into her purse for her invitation. "Do you need to see the invite? I know the party is by invitation only."

Liz shook her head. "I know you're on the list. Let me just check which table you've been assigned to."

"Assigned tables?" Mandy repeated and Liz nodded, her eyes on the iPad in front of her.

"There are so many guests that Leo's mother felt it was necessary to do a seating chart. Okay, here you are. Table twenty-five. All the tables are numbered tonight so you should find it pretty easily. Make your way to the right. There's a buffet dinner set out—you'll see it. Grab a plate and find your seat. I think Gabriel's going to speak during dessert."

Mandy and Ashley found their table quickly and then went through the buffet line.

"It's not noticeable that I'm looking around for Leo, is it?" she whispered into Ashley's ear.

Ashley grinned. "Of course not. I think the family is all seated together. Look past our table, farther to the right."

Ashley was right. Gabriel Romano sat at the head of a long table that seated maybe twenty people. But Leo was nowhere to be seen.

The girls went back to their table and were quickly joined

by a man who introduced himself as the Romano family attorney, along with his wife and two members of Leo's staff. Mandy noticed a woman with a camera taking a steady stream of shots, and assumed she was a professional photographer.

"Look!" Ashley said, pointing to a satellite table near the family. "That's the mayor. I saw him on TV last night!"

"He must be a friend of Gabriel's," Mandy surmised, her eyes scanning the rest of the room. "Oh, wow, Ash. That's Giovanni De Benedetti over to the left!"

"Who's that?"

"Only one of the most respected chefs in this country!"

Ashley shrugged. "Oh. Cool. Have you tried this chicken Alfredo? It's to die for."

With difficulty, Mandy turned her attention away from the myriad guests and onto her plate of pasta.

Leo checked the dessert trays before the staff took them to the dining room. While many of his father's long-standing staff were at the party as guests, Leo had also arranged for several waitstaff to come in to serve. Adam was running the kitchen tonight. Leo nodded his approval of the dessert trays and the platters went up on the shoulders of the servers as they filed out of the kitchen.

Leo made his way back to the dining room. Thankfully, his father was having a good day. He seemed energized by the guests. As Leo weaved through the tables, stopping to shake hands with friends and family, the sight of unruly, wavy brown hair distracted him.

Mandy.

As usual, his composure wavered when he saw her. He walked to her table and leaned over her shoulder.

"Chicken Alfredo? Tsk-tsk. I asked Adam to bring out the Lobster Magnifico just for you, Ms. Seymour."

He could see the flush on her neck before she even turned to look at him.

"Leo, this is my friend Ashley. Ash, this is Leo."

"Well, well. Leonardo Romano. I've heard lots about you!" Mandy's friend spoke with a thick Southern drawl.

Leo straightened and reached over to shake hands with Ashley. He glanced at his father's table and caught his mother looking at him. With a smile, she waved at him to stay where he was. After saying a quick hello to his father's attorney, Leo pulled up a chair next to Mandy.

"You look beautiful, Mandy," he said in a low voice. Her smile lit up her eyes.

"You don't have to stay here with us, Leo. You should be with your family," Mandy insisted.

And you should be with me.

Leo shrugged. "I'll go back in a minute. You're an honored guest tonight, Mandy. We've all read your article. My mother basically wept."

At that, Mandy blushed again.

"She cried?"

"She did. Thank you so much for what you wrote. The tribute was really beautiful." The words came easily to Leo. He only hoped Mandy understood how earnest they were.

"Liz mentioned that your father is going to speak during dessert," Mandy said.

"Yes, if he's feeling up to it. The dessert trays have been added to the buffet table, but in a moment, we'll actually bring out a large Italian wedding cake in honor of my father's retirement. Once we cut the cake, I believe coffee will be served and he'll want to thank all his guests. There's a microphone and a stand for him near the table."

"May I take your photo?"

Mandy and Leo both looked up as the photographer stood in front of them, holding her camera. Leo had little doubt this photo op was prearranged by either his mother or Isa. Mandy looked at him, her eyebrows raised.

"Of course," Leo agreed, moving closer to Mandy as they both smiled for the photographer. He eased back away once the photographer left, though he wished he didn't have to.

"Leo!" Isa called out from the head table.

Leo spoke reluctantly, "I have to go. It's probably time for the cake."

Mandy nodded. "That's all right, Leo."

Leo lowered his voice. "Mandy, we really need to talk—"

"Leonardo!" Leo recognized the rising impatience in Isa's tone and stood up.

"This is not the right time. But soon, I have things I need to say," he told Mandy before he made his way through the crowd.

When he got to the family's table, Isa grabbed his arm. "I think Dad's too tired to stand. And he's shaking," she said in almost a whisper. "Bring the microphone over to where he's sitting, that way he won't feel obligated to stand."

Leo nodded and did as she requested. He waited to the side as his parents stood together and cut the cake, then joined in the applause. Once his father was seated, Leo brought him the microphone.

"Everyone can hear you with this, Dad. You don't need to stand." His father looked ready to argue, but then he conceded. Leo could see his dad's right hand tremble badly, so he held the microphone for him.

"Thank you all so much for coming," Gabriel said, his eyes glistening. "This has been a night of celebration. I want to thank God for all He's given me—my family, my work, my friends. I want to thank Mandy Seymour for her lovely article announcing my retirement."

Leo's gaze shot to where Mandy was sitting. When her eyes met his, Leo sensed the weight of all the things he needed to say to her. He felt the unmistakable pull toward her that came over him every time he was near her.

"I also want to ask you all to continue to offer my son, Leonardo, the support you have offered me throughout the years. I am so proud of him. He has taken on a very large responsibility, and to show our gratitude, his sister, his mother and I have a gift for him."

His dad pulled an envelope from his jacket pocket and handed it to him. Leo blinked in surprise.

"We all know that the life of a chef is a demanding one. But life, my son, is more important than work. I want you to work to *live,* not to live to work. And so we want to make sure you take a break every now and then."

Leo opened the envelope and pulled out a plane ticket to Italy. He leaned down and hugged his father, then his mother, and finally Isa.

"Thank you," Leo said.

"You've earned it," his mother said with pride in her eyes.

His father held up a goblet of sparkling water for a toast. "To my son!" he called out.

"Salute!" the crowd responded.

When Mandy saw an opening, she rushed forward to talk to Gabriel. While she didn't want to take any time away from his family, she couldn't leave without speaking to him.

"Mandy!" His face lit up when he saw her. She noticed how fatigued he looked. Mandy leaned down and hugged him.

"Gabriel, I'm so thrilled you liked the article."

He reached forward and took her hand in his. "It was perfect. I knew it would be."

"Well, I appreciate your faith in me."

"It meant so much to all of us." His gaze turned to where Leo stood talking with a group of people. "But to me especially."

Mandy stepped back. "I don't want to keep you, but I wanted to thank you for inviting me. Not just tonight." Mandy hoped he understood her meaning. She felt as though Gabriel had invited her into his life, into his family.

"We'll see you soon, Mandy," he said with confidence.

That confident tone stayed with her all the way back to Ashley's.

"What did you think of Leo?" Mandy asked before Ashley got out of the car. Ashley reached for the door handle.

"I think he's great, Mandy. Gorgeous, nice, sweet, good company and…"

"And?" Mandy prodded.

"And most importantly—" Ashley looked at Mandy "—I think he's 100 percent in love with you."

Mandy shook her head. "Oh, sure. That's why he keeps telling me he can't be in a relationship with me."

"Mandy, you should see the way he looks at you."

Mandy remembered her mother saying almost the same thing.

"How does he look at me?" she wondered, hating that she couldn't keep from asking. Ashley smiled.

"Well, for one thing—when was the guy *not* looking at you? When you talk, Mandy, it's like he's absorbing every word. He notices every move you make. And from where I was sitting, it was so glaringly obvious that he sees the real you, Mandy. The one I see. The one everyone sees… but you, I think."

Mandy couldn't answer.

"Listen to me. I know you're afraid," Ashley said gently. "I know you've had this perception of yourself for as long as you can remember. It stems from your mother and a whole lot of other issues. But it's not who you are, and this is important, Mandy, it's not who you *ever were.* You were *never* a failure, *never* inadequate or mediocre. *Never* pathetic or insignificant. We've been friends a long time. Long enough for me to know you've felt all those things at one time or another. But feeling them doesn't make them true, honey."

Mandy's breath caught, and for a moment, the silence seemed to zero in on her and everything else melted away. Ashley's words covered her like a balm.

"It's time to see yourself for who you are. And if you can't do that yet, start by seeing who Christ is *in* you."

"I have been trying," Mandy acknowledged. "I do want to see myself as God sees me, Ash. It's just not easy for me."

Ashley squeezed Mandy's hand. "I know, sweet pea. Just keep reminding yourself that you're loved with an everlasting love."

"God loves me with an everlasting love," Mandy repeated, her eyes suddenly welling up with tears.

"That's right. And that's an incredible kind of love."

Mandy nodded. "It's the kind of love that gives you confidence." She'd tried to convince herself of all of those same things hundreds of times over the years. But in that moment Mandy recognized a new sensation churning in her heart, an almost startling certainty—she was ready to believe those words were true.

Early Monday morning, Mandy woke to a snow-covered Denver, not unusual for early spring in Colorado. She quickly determined that it was a work-from-home kind of morning and settled in front of her laptop, wearing her pajamas and sipping English breakfast tea. Her cell rang, interrupting her latest review. Mandy's heart rate doubled at the sight of the name on her caller ID. Bernice St. James.

"Mandy, I hope you have some good news for me!" her voice chimed.

Mandy sat silent for a moment. One thought invaded her consciousness.

I have loved you with an everlasting love.

A feeling of calm spread through Mandy.

I haven't forgotten, Lord.
Mandy closed her laptop, her decision made.

Leo rubbed his weary eyes as he padded through his apartment. Exhausted or not, the party had been a success and Leo was thankful for that. From his kitchen, he clicked on the television, at once hearing reports of the six inches of snow that had fallen during the night.

I need a day off.

Leo looked at the ticket to Italy sitting on his kitchen counter. His parents had booked it for the last week in September but told him he could change the dates to whenever best suited him. Leo slid the ticket into one of the kitchen drawers.

I can't even think about traveling anytime soon.

But his father's words from the night before drifted around in his thoughts.

Work to live. Don't live to work. Life is the most important thing.

Leo poured a bowl of cereal, too tired to cook anything. His mind was inundated with images from the night before. One thing had stuck with him all through the night—the truth that, without a doubt, the success of his father's life was seen in the group of people who surrounded him to show their care and support. His dad had touched so many lives. None more than Leo's.

Leo walked to the kitchen window and looked out at the few stray snowflakes drifting down.

That's the success I want. That's the sort of life I want.

And whatever his life entailed, Leo knew one thing: he wanted Mandy to be part of it.

Chapter 18

Tuesday afternoon, Leo wrote Mandy an email, asking her if they could have dinner together Thursday evening. He'd checked his email off and on for three hours, restless as he waited for Mandy's answer. When a letter finally showed up in his inbox, Leo dropped everything to read the one-line email from Mandy. Yes. My turn to choose: my apartment at 7:30 sharp. Be there.

By the time Thursday rolled around, Leo still had no idea what he was going to say to Mandy. He knew he needed to communicate to her how deep his feelings were for her, but just *how* he would do that eluded him. Snow had fallen on Denver for two days straight, so Thursday afternoon, Leo spent fifteen minutes scraping ice and snow from the windshield of his car.

Leo pulled into the empty parking lot at the Franklin location. He was relieved to see that the lot had already been cleared of the snow. He entered through the kitchen door and turned lights on as he made his way down the hallway to his office. When he flipped the light switch and opened the door, his mouth fell open and he dropped his keys to the floor.

Mom.

Leo scrambled to grab his keys and then just stood in

the doorway, taking in the scene that was his office. His mother had done a complete overhaul. His father's large, bulky furniture had been replaced by sleek black bookshelves, a simple black desk and two cream-colored leather chairs. The colorful walls were now white, with symmetrical black-and-white framed photos filling the wall space. Leo moved closer to inspect the photos and his heart ached once he saw the pictures his mother had chosen.

An enlarged photo of Leo and his father stood out from the center. Leo couldn't have been more than three years old in the photo. He had a chunk of bread in his hands and he was being held by his father's strong, healthy arms. Gabriel was laughing, his face full of happiness. Most of the photos were of Leo and his family. Some were taken during their years at the Los Angeles Romano's. Some were photos taken during family vacations in Italy at Leo's great-grandmother's villa. Every photo stirred an emotional memory.

On the adjacent wall, in bold, cursive black letters, these words had been painted:

Jesus said to them: Come and dine.
—John 21:12

The office could not have been more perfect. It occurred to Leo how well his mother knew him. While the office decor seemed much more in line with the Fifteenth Street location, this was *his* space, Leo's space. His mother had turned the office into a reflection of Leo and made it a place that he could own.

Leo hung his jacket behind the door and sat at his desk, where one last surprise awaited him.

At the corner of his desk rested a small framed photo, also black-and-white. Leo took the photo in his hands and studied the people in the picture—himself and Mandy. It was the photo taken at his father's party. He stared at Mandy's unruly hair, her beautiful smile, her composure that always seemed to tame his anxiety.

Leo set the picture back in its place, right where it belonged.

Mandy wanted to cry. She looked at the mess that was her kitchen and sat down right on the floor.

Insisting on dinner at my house was obviously not my brightest moment.

Her great intentions to cook Leo one of her fabulous-but-untried recipes from the Food Network had turned out to be disastrous. The breading wouldn't stick, the supposedly fresh lettuce she'd bought looked limp, she'd had no idea she was out of vinegar until it was too late, and the dessert needed to set overnight in the refrigerator—a small detail she'd somehow overlooked in the recipe.

The fan over the stove ran loudly; Mandy's attempt to suck out the smell of burned bread crumbs. With an hour before Leo was slated to arrive, Mandy gave up.

There's no way I'm serving this inedible mush to an accomplished chef. What was I thinking?

Am I trying to make Leo turn around and run? I should've known that a little luck in the kitchen would be more than I should hope for.

With an exasperated groan, Mandy pulled herself up off the floor and tried to decide which to do first: order takeout or clean the kitchen.

Takeout.

After placing an order to the Peking Duck down the street, she rolled up her sleeves and prepared to work a miracle in her apartment.

At least I can trust the Peking Duck to provide the best Chinese food in Denver.

Mandy froze in her steps.

What if Leo doesn't like Chinese food?

She shook away the thought. Everyone liked Chinese food. And since she'd just spent $50 on rice and shrimp and dumplings—he'd just have to like it. She concentrated on mopping the kitchen floor and wiping down the counters, hiding the trash filled with burnt-to-a-crisp crumbs out on the back patio, and vacuuming the area rug. She lit candles all around the living room and turned on her favorite instrumental CD. Since her kitchen table was so small, Mandy decided to serve dinner at the coffee table.

Good thing I vacuumed the rug.

With ten minutes to spare, her huge paper bag of Chinese food arrived via teenage boy, giving her just enough time to set out the food and make everything look pretty.

The doorbell rang just as Mandy set fortune cookies by each plate.

She paused to wipe the sweat from her forehead and fan herself.

Okay, you've been going nonstop for hours. Time to relax and have Chinese food.

With Leo.

Since the day he'd brought breakfast to her workplace, Mandy could tell that Leo was doing his best to be friends with her without asking for more. He emailed often and asked about her work. He kept her updated about his dad's condition. But something had shifted the night of Gabriel's retirement party. She'd sensed it in the way Leo talked to her and looked at her, and when she'd received the email from him asking her to have dinner with him, she felt it even more strongly.

Her nerves didn't subside so she just opened the front door and there stood Leo. Her heart did that flip-flop thing it seemed incapable of *not* doing in Leo's presence. He held out a bouquet of white roses.

"Thanks, Leo." His smile matched her own.

She graciously took the flowers and found a vase for them while Leo looked around the apartment. Granted, that took him all of half a minute.

Mandy wiped her hands on a dish towel and motioned toward the boxes of Chinese food.

"I was going to cook," she began apologetically, but Leo shook his head as he took off his jacket and draped it over the sofa.

"Don't worry about it. Chinese food is perfect. And I can't wait to see what you ordered for us."

Mandy threw two pillows onto the rug for them to sit on and they sat cross-legged on either side of the coffee table, facing each other.

"We've got fried dumplings to start with, and shrimp fried rice, General Tso's chicken, and beef and broccoli. I was hungry so I ordered a little bit of everything," Mandy said sheepishly.

Leo picked up chopsticks and reached for the carton of dumplings. "Sounds good to me."

"So when are you going to Italy?" Mandy asked as she opened the box of shrimp fried rice.

Leo hesitated.

"The ticket your parents gave you?" Mandy reminded him and he nodded as though it had just dawned on him.

"Right. Well, that's sort of up in the air. Maybe in September, but I doubt it. I was thinking more like next spring. I like Italy in the spring. Have you ever been?"

Mandy shook her head. "No. It's on my list, though."

"List?" Leo echoed.

Mandy handed him the box of rice and opened a Styrofoam container of beef and broccoli. With relief, she noticed that the tangy aromas of the Chinese food adequately drowned out the smell of burnt bread.

"Yeah, my list. You know, my list of things to see, places to go, things to accomplish."

"Oh, I see."

Mandy reached for her chopsticks. "What's on your list?"

"Well…I've always wanted to go sky diving."

Mandy shuddered. "Terrifying. *So* not on my list."

Leo chuckled. "What else is on your list?"

"I want to ice skate in Central Park in December."

Leo smiled. "That's a good one."

They ate quietly for a moment, then Mandy broke the silence. "I was glad you asked to have dinner with me, Leo."

"I've missed you, Mandy," he said and she drew in a sharp breath.

I think the vibe between us just raced over the friendship border.

"I've missed you, too. At the party the other night, you said you needed to talk to me. I'm listening, Leo." Mandy waited, hope rising up inside her too fast for her to squelch it.

Leo wiped his mouth and set aside his napkin. He looked directly at her. "I've changed my mind, Mandy. And I know that sounds immature and childish. And I want you to know that I have no expectations of you, but…things have changed for me."

"What things?" Mandy wondered.

"In here." Leo held his hand over his heart. "Really, my circumstances haven't changed—*I've* changed."

Mandy tried to swallow. But he was looking at her with those dark eyes of his—in that way only he could. "I see," she forced herself to say. "And what have you changed your mind about?"

"Several things. I've stopped blaming God for my dad's illness. I've stopped doubting my decision to keep the restaurants. And I've changed my mind about us. I'd like for us to be in a relationship. I want that more than anything else, Mandy."

Oh Lord, what do I say? You know what I want to say. What do You want me to say?

Mandy set down her chopsticks.

"I'm afraid you'll change your mind again," she confessed.

"I won't." Leo's confident tone reminded her of Gabriel. He reached across the table and took both her hands in his. "And once you're working for Take Me There, I'll support you 100 percent. I'll miss you when you're gone, but I know it's a great opportunity. I'm behind you all the way."

Mandy appreciated his words more than he could know. She let go of his hands, picked up her chopsticks, her pulse slowed and she relaxed. She looked down for a moment. "Thank you for saying that, Leo. But you should know I've decided only to do occasional freelance jobs for Take Me There. I'm not going to be joining them full-time." Mandy peeked back up at Leo; he looked stunned.

"Why not?"

"I'm happy where I am. Plus…going to interesting places by myself isn't all that appealing."

Mandy watched as relief filled Leo's face. "I have to admit, the thought of you being away so much—well, let me just say that I don't want us to be apart like that."

Mandy took a deep breath. "I want to believe that, Leo."

"Mandy, please give me the chance to prove it to you. Please. Even if only for my family's sake, who are desperate for us to be together," Leo begged. At that comment, Mandy laughed. Leo smiled. He leaned over the coffee table and touched Mandy's face before pressing his lips to hers in a kiss that begged for more.

After a moment, Mandy pulled back, trying to clear her head, at the same time hoping she never lost that delicious, fragile feeling that came over her whenever Leo kissed her.

"For your family's sake, huh?" she teased.

"For my sake. I am desperate to be with you."

Mandy didn't say anything for a moment.

"Mandy?" Leo said with concern. He gently lifted her chin until their eyes met. "What's wrong?"

Mandy tried to shake away her feelings and just enjoy the moment, but she couldn't.

"Leo, what do you like about me?"

He stared at her for a moment.

"I need to hear it from you," she said quietly.

Leo stood up, reached for Mandy's hand and led her to the sofa where they sat down next to each other.

"Mandy, as far as I can tell, there isn't anything I *don't* like about you. But if you want to know specifics—I like the way I feel when I'm with you. Everything can be chaotic around me, but when I'm with you, I feel like I can handle it. I think you're beautiful. I think you're an incredibly talented writer. So many things attract me to you—your faith, your easy way of getting along with people, your heart for helping others."

Mandy absorbed Leo's words. They seemed to run over her and through her, filling her with confidence.

"And there's something else I want you to know, Mandy. Something really important."

"What's that?" Mandy asked. Leo sighed and leaned close enough to Mandy that their foreheads touched. He closed his eyes.

"You can ask me what I like about you as many times as you want to, as many times as you need to. I'll never get tired of answering."

"Really?" Mandy whispered.

"Positively," Leo answered just before he kissed her again. A deep, lingering kiss that both of them seemed reluctant to end.

Happiness filled every inch of Mandy. "So our next date is your choice, Leo. Where are we going?"

Chapter 19

Mandy poured two cups of hot tea and handed one to Ashley.

"So, I've lost you forever," Ashley bemoaned. "Not that I'm complaining or anything."

Mandy stirred a spoonful of sugar into her cup. "Are you serious? Haven't you been the one pushing me toward Leo ever since the moment we met?"

Ashley ignored Mandy's questions. "I've barely seen you for the past month!"

Mandy opened her refrigerator, searching for cream for her tea. "That's funny. I keep thinking I saw you at Bible study two days ago."

"You haven't even asked me to be a bridesmaid," Ashley pouted.

Mandy nearly choked from laughing. "That's because there's been zero talk of marriage! We've been dating steadily for six weeks, Ashley. No one's getting married right now."

"Fine. But once we start talking about it, I want you to know my expectation."

Mandy suppressed her amusement. "Thank you for the warning."

"Speaking of marriage, has the boy told you he loves you yet?" Ashley asked bluntly. Mandy shook her head.

"No, but neither of us is in a rush, Ash."

"Well, somebody oughta be. Biological clock and all."

Mandy rolled her eyes. Ashley sat at the kitchen table and Mandy sat across from her.

"Mandy, in all seriousness, do you want to marry him? Are you in love with him?" Ashley's eyes were wide with curiosity.

Mandy shrugged and sipped her tea. "Maybe."

"Maybe! What kind of an answer is that?" Ashley screeched.

"The only kind you're going to get," Mandy retorted.

Ashley paused and gave Mandy a sly smile. "You're forgetting my incredible powers of persuasion."

"You're right. I should just give you an answer now to skip all the hassle," Mandy agreed.

"My point exactly."

"I love him. I *think* he loves me. As for whether I would like to marry him, I need to pray about that."

Ashley sat back, crestfallen. "How can I argue with that?"

"You can't," Mandy replied jovially.

Leo finished going through both restaurants' payrolls and then reviewed his marketing expenses. He carefully examined the outgoing expenditures of each restaurant and then analyzed the profits. Two of his younger waiters had resigned because of college schedules, so Leo needed to hire new people. He checked the clock, knowing he was running the Fifteenth Street kitchen that evening since Jeremy was on vacation. He finished his paperwork and headed toward the kitchen. The restaurant was already buzzing with staff preparing for the evening.

Leo walked into the kitchen and put on his apron. The

smell of bread baking competed with the aroma coming from the stoves where enormous pots of soup simmered.

"What's our special tonight, Margo?" he asked his sous chef.

She tied her apron around her waist. "Spinach artichoke pizza with goat cheese. One of my kids' favorites."

Leo inspected the freshly washed spinach. "Sounds good. Thanks, Margo."

"Hey, chef." Angelina clocked in.

"Angie, I thought you were off tonight."

Angelina shrugged. "Dana asked me to cover for her. Something came up with her family tonight. So here I am."

"Good. Isa's supposed to be coming in tonight with her boyfriend for the first time."

"Gotcha. I'll take care of them." Angelina washed her hands and dried them on a towel, then leaned against the kitchen counter. "How are things with Mandy?"

Leo tied a bandanna around his head to keep his hair out of his eyes. "Everything's fine, Angie."

"Glad to hear it."

Angelina disappeared out of the kitchen and Leo turned to his work station.

Things were more than fine, if Leo were honest. Every moment he spent with Mandy only confirmed his feelings for her. He felt certain she felt the same way. But every time he started to think about marriage, old thoughts of his broken engagement plagued his mind. He recognized that he wanted to marry Mandy, he just told himself it wasn't the right time yet.

Leo knew that his relationship with Mandy didn't mirror his relationship with Carol Ann. The maturity, the friendship, the deep respect he felt when it came to Mandy took their relationship to an entirely different level.

He knew it was the sort of relationship that could end in the kind of marriage he'd always hoped for. Why, then, did old fears resurface whenever he wanted to broach the topic with her?

As the staff continued to fill the kitchen and the dinner rush began, Leo set aside thoughts of Mandy and marriage and poured himself into cooking.

By the time Leo dragged himself out to his car that night after eleven o'clock, he felt too exhausted to think of anything. For some reason, he felt the urge to drive to his parents' home and sleep in his old room. He jingled the keys in his pocket. Why not? His mother would be thrilled to see him at breakfast. Leo switched lanes and drove to the Romano family home.

He parked in the driveway and used his house key to go inside. Something about the familiar place always comforted him. He dropped his coat on the sofa and headed to the stairs.

"Leo?"

Leo's hair stood on end at the sound of his father's voice. He noticed a light on in the kitchen and walked in that direction.

"Dad, it's me. I hope I didn't alarm you. I just felt like waking up here at home tomorrow. You know, letting mom cook me breakfast."

His father sat at the kitchen table, an old scrapbook open in front of him. "She'll be thrilled. You go on up and get some sleep."

But Leo pulled out a chair and sat next to his dad. "Why are you up?"

"Insomnia, unfortunately. I'm not sleeping well these days. I didn't want to disturb your mother. I started looking through some old photos, reminiscing. It's the kind of thing old people enjoy doing," he said wryly.

Leo glanced at his father's trembling hands. "It's the kind of thing I enjoy, too. Let me take a look." He pulled the scrapbook in his direction and flipped through the pages of old photos from his dad's childhood. He turned to a page full of his parents' wedding photos.

"That was the best day of my life," his father told him. "Well, one of them. The days that you and Isa were born were like none other. You know, we're all hoping to hear wedding bells for you sooner rather than later, Leo."

Leo stared down at the wedding photos, studying his parents' blissful smiles. "Don't get me wrong, I want to marry Mandy, Dad. It's just…well, the last time I wanted to get married, things didn't end so well." Leo sat back and crossed his arms.

His dad closed the scrapbook. "She wasn't the right one for you, Leonardo. If you feel as though God is telling you that Mandy *is* the right one, don't be afraid. What have I always told you? *Taste and see that the Lord is good.* Leo, his plans for you are good. Trust him. Do you love Mandy?"

"More than anything. To be completely honest…" Leo lowered his voice. "I love her more than I ever loved Carol Ann. The way I feel about Mandy—I don't know. It's like nothing I've ever felt before. I know God brought Mandy into my life. I know she's the one I'm supposed to be with."

His dad smiled. "Then ask her to marry you."

Gabriel stood slowly and Leo helped him, supporting him as they climbed the stairs together.

"Your mother and I will be moving our things down to the first floor tomorrow. We should have done it sooner. The stairs are too much for me. We'll be moving into the guest room. Your mother spent the past two days turning the guest room into our new master bedroom. She's so gifted when it comes to things like that. You should take a look at it tomorrow."

The thought of his parents moving out of the room they'd shared for so many years was a sad one for Leo. But he knew it was necessary.

"I'll help you move everything down tomorrow," Leo

promised him. His father leaned against him, his frame a little thinner and weaker than Leo had noticed of late.

"I know you will, son."

After his father had disappeared into his parents' bedroom, Leo headed to his old bedroom across the hallway. He lay awake in the same double bed he'd slept in as a teenager and prayed.

God, help me help my Dad. Give me the strength to be strong for him. And give me the courage to follow my heart and offer all that I have, all that I am to Mandy. I need her in a way that I've never needed anyone before.

The next day Mandy winked at Leo as they passed each other in the hallway of his parents' home. She'd been thrilled when he'd texted her, asking her to join him as he moved furniture from upstairs to the first-floor bedroom.

Mandy carried a vase downstairs and found Rosalinda in the kitchen.

"Rosalinda? Did you want this in the bedroom? Isa asked me to bring it down."

She looked up with a smile. "Yes. You know, that's a vase my mother-in-law gave me. I was so nervous to bring it home on the plane. I held it in my lap for hours."

"It's lovely," Mandy agreed, holding it even tighter.

"Why don't you set it on the nightstand in the new bedroom and then come help me with dinner?"

Mandy grinned. "I would love to."

A few minutes later, Mandy joined Rosalinda in the kitchen, pausing to wash her hands and slip on one of the many aprons hanging near the pantry.

"What are we making?" Mandy asked.

"Gabriel's asked for pesto chicken Florentine for dinner. It's one of Isa's favorites. Leo makes it best, though. But as he's moving furniture, I shall cook, with your help."

"My mother used to say that cooking for her family was one of her greatest pleasures," Mandy said.

Rosalinda smiled with agreement and understanding. "It's true for me, too."

Mandy sautéed garlic before adding strips of chicken to the hot pan, while Leo's mother created the pesto sauce. They cooked and laughed together until Leo came into the kitchen.

"I'm starving. Is dinner almost ready?"

His mother swatted at his hand as Leo reached for a chunk of bread. "Let me go check on your father. Yes, dinner is ready. Your Mandy has helped me."

Rosalinda left the kitchen, and Leo and Mandy set the table for dinner.

"My Mandy," Leo repeated with a twinkle in his eyes. Mandy loved the sound of that.

Chapter 20

Mandy reread the last two paragraphs of her article about a new Japanese restaurant in Castle Rock, Colorado, pushed the save button and closed the document. She stretched and leaned back away from her desk. The clock on the wall reminded her that it was after five o'clock and time to leave the office. Leo would be working by now. She knew he was running the Fifteenth Street kitchen all week.

Mandy gathered her things and turned the light off in her office. As she drove home, she thought of Leo.

Lord, does he want to marry me? I know without a doubt that Leo's the one for me. But does he know that yet? If not, could you maybe help him along with that?

Mandy picked up her mail before taking the elevator to her condo. Once inside, she dropped the stack of magazines and bills onto the coffee table. From the middle of the stack, a small postcard fell to the floor. She set aside her purse and jacket and loosened the scarf around her neck before picking it up.

She read the word ALASKA in bright red letters in one corner; a picture of a whale jumping in the ocean covered the postcard. Mandy flipped it over.

Mandy,
I'm in our room on the ship right now, about to dress for dinner. But I had to tell you. I saw a whale today!

More than one, actually. I was standing on a boat, mist from the water spraying over me, watching these gorgeous creatures, wishing you could see them, too, and I felt it. I felt His favor over me, Mandy. It was indescribable.

   We love you and wish you were here! Can't wait to show you all our pictures!
Love,
Mom

Mandy used a magnet to display the postcard on her refrigerator. She stood in front of it, just staring at that whale, a splash of joy coursing through her. In that moment, Mandy felt her mother's favor over her, something she'd never experienced before. And it blessed her.

And she felt it, too. Along with God's healing and gift of reconciliation, she felt his favor over her. A stillness surrounded her and Mandy closed her eyes.

If I have Your favor, Lord, then I can be patient waiting for Leo's. If I have You, I know the rest will fall into place.

After the longest week of his life, Leo's relief at turning the kitchen over to Jeremy was clear.

"Can't take the heat anymore?" Jeremy teased after his first night back at work. Leo laughed good-naturedly.

"Only in small doses. Running the kitchen and overseeing the restaurants is more than I can handle on an ongoing basis. That's why I'm thankful for you, buddy." Leo patted Jeremy on his back.

"Mandy wouldn't be a factor now, would she?" Jeremy grinned. Leo shrugged but he knew Jeremy was right. He hadn't spent any real time with Mandy all week and he missed her.

"Okay, chef, everything's ready," Angie said, pushing through the kitchen door.

"What about the meal?" Leo asked. Jeremy pointed to the cooler.

"I set aside two dishes. There's plenty of salad as well and a few desserts for you to choose from."

Leo clapped his hands. "Excellent. Thanks, guys. Now get out of here."

The rest of the staff filed out the kitchen door and Leo checked his watch. He'd asked Mandy to join him for an extra-late dinner after closing. He turned around at the sound of a tap-tap-tap on the kitchen door. As the last waiter left, Mandy walked through the open door.

"You made it." Leo walked over and pulled Mandy into a hug. She rested her head against his shoulder.

"I've missed you, chef."

He tilted her chin up to face him and kissed her softly.

"I've missed you, too. Let's eat, you must be hungry. I'm sorry you had to wait so late."

Mandy set her things on the counter and pulled up one of the bar stools in the kitchen but Leo shook his head and took her hand, leading her out to the dining room.

"No, no. We're eating in style tonight."

Mandy gasped when they reached their table and Leo's grin widened. Angelina had fixed up one table for two with special china Leo had borrowed from his mother. Two candlesticks glowed in the center of the table and a small vase of fresh flowers gave the table a display of color. A bottle of sparkling cider chilled in a bucket of ice on a side table and Leo filled two goblets for them, then pulled out a chair for Mandy.

"Have a seat," he told her.

"Let me help you bring out our meal," Mandy objected, but Leo shook his head, insisting she sit down.

"Tonight, I'm serving you, Mandy," he said simply before heading back to the kitchen. Once the food was properly heated, Leo lifted the serving tray over his shoulder, memories of his years as a server running through his mind. Mandy giggled as she watched him come toward her with the tray and then set the food on their table. After praying over the meal, Leo took a bite of spaghetti Bolognese, realizing how hungry he was. He hadn't eaten all day—too nervous.

"Jeremy cooked the meal," Leo admitted. "I wanted to make you something extra special, but—"

Mandy held up her hand. "Stop there. Everything about this night is perfect, Leo." Her tone allowed for no argument. The light from the candles flickered across Mandy's face and Leo felt overwhelmed by how beautiful she looked. She tore a piece of bread in half and handed one piece to him, the way he often did for her.

Leo tried to steady his breathing and slow his heart rate, but his nerves wouldn't settle down.

After dinner, he brought out two slices of cheesecake and a pot of coffee for the two of them. He sat silently as Mandy told him all about her mother's postcard and how much it meant to her. He loved the shine in her eyes and the happiness in her voice. Usually, he would feel content to just listen to Mandy talk, but not tonight. He felt the pressure of all the things he needed to say. Inside him there was an intense urging to have nothing left unsaid between them by the end of this night.

As Mandy poured coffee for them both, Leo knew the moment was right.

"Mandy, there's something I've been thinking about for quite some time. Something I've wanted to talk about with you."

"Okay," she said. "Tell me."

"I'm in love with you."

The words came out more bluntly and quickly than he'd intended. But there they were.

There's no going back now.

Mandy's eyes widened and she set down the coffeepot.

"Are you sure?" she asked and he smiled easily, relieved to finally have said the words he'd felt for months.

"I'm sure."

Leo watched as Mandy swallowed with difficulty. He could see her eyes welling up. "In that case," she said with a small smile and a definite catch in her voice, "I'm absolutely in love with you, too."

In that moment, he knew that whatever had broken inside of him when Carol Ann left had mended completely.

"Say that again, Mandy, if you don't mind."

Mandy's smiled widened. "I love you, Leo." Her words came effortlessly.

"Then will you marry me?"

One tear cascaded down Mandy's face and Leo reached over to wipe it away.

"Yes," she whispered.

Leo stood up, reached for Mandy's hand and pulled her up next to him, where he sealed that agreement with a kiss.

He thought of the ticket his parents had given him. He would need to buy another one.

"Mandy?"

She wiped her eyes and smiled. "What?"

"I'm just thinking of our honeymoon."

Mandy laughed. "Already?"

Leo leaned down to kiss her again. "How does a table for two in Italy sound?"

Mandy pressed one finger to her lips and pretended to think it over. "It sounds like a worthy choice to me."

* * * * *